Rishabh Puri is an entrepreneur of Indian origin with businesses in Nigeria, Dubai and China. He owns a record label and is also a movie producer. Despite his demanding day job, he finds time to indulge in his passion for writing fiction. He is a national bestselling author with four books penned under his name - *Inside the Heart of Hope*, *Flying Without Wings*, *Seductive Affair* and *Aavya*. His readers have loved and enjoyed all his books immensely, and *Forever Yours* is his fifth book.

Rishabh has taught himself to live life to the fullest, against all odds, despite what life has to offer him. His writings too are mostly centred on the beauty of hope, love and life. Rishabh is also an avid traveller and a supercar enthusiast. He is based in Lagos, Nigeria and Dubai, UAE currently, but visits India regularly, returning to his birthplace Chandigarh, which remains immensely close to his heart.

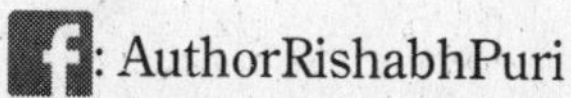

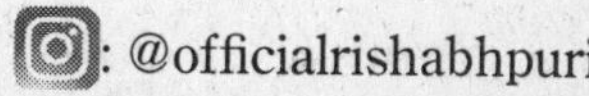

Forever Yours

Rishabh Puri

Srishti
PUBLISHERS & DISTRIBUTORS

Srishti Publishers & Distributors
Registered Office: N-16, C.R. Park
New Delhi – 110 019
Corporate Office: 212A, Peacock Lane
Shahpur Jat, New Delhi – 110 049
editorial@srishtipublishers.com

First published by
Srishti Publishers & Distributors in 2019

10 9 8 7 6 5 4 3 2 1

This is a work of fiction. The characters, places, organisations and events described in this book are either a work of the author's imagination or have been used fictitiously. Any resemblance to people, living or dead, places, events, communities or organisations is purely coincidental.

Printed and bound in India

Acknowledgement

Love is the greatest certainty this life has to offer, but life happens where love's details get hazy. The love you want and think you deserve might not be the love that saves you in the end. But, looking back on a life of blessings, I see now that at every turn, love was with me, in many forms, hand in hand.

First and foremost, I'd like to thank God for the overwhelming blessings He has graced me with, being made from love and showing nothing but love to His whole creation. I would also like to thank my mother, father, and sister for their love and support throughout my whole life. This foundation of love and unconditional acceptance has been the firmest footing I've ever known, and it allows me to fly.

The doctors who have, through their love of their art, taken on a case as difficult as mine and made it their own. Dr Alok Suryavanshi, my heart surgeon, my brother. My life has been in your hands so many times, and you have never shied away from the challenge of keeping me going. Dr. Dennis Lox, your seemingly boundless knowledge is matched only by the sense of humour that was able to lift my spirits from their lowest point. Without these doctors, I would not have had the life in my body to put pen to page. To Dr Eliot Brinton, my gratitude for the years of study and expertise that led me to you is beyond what words can communicate. Your work has changed my life for the better. I am beyond grateful. And Dr Dinesh Nair, I cannot thank you enough, for not only being one of the best cardiologists, but for being the most caring, gentle, and understanding person I could have asked for. You never seemed to be in a hurry and showed true concern. And, of course, your smile; it would brighten up anyone's day.

Finally, I am grateful to you, my dearest reader, who loves words and loves stories about love. Whether this is the first of my books you've ever picked up or you are a devoted fan, you bring my dreams to life each day, and I hold you warmly in my heart. I hope you enjoy this book.

1

Kabir

"You really think we should go?" My mother fussed over me as she stood in the doorway. I shot a look at my father, imploring him to help me out here and allow me a bit of space. He took her arm and nodded to me.

"I think we need to give Kabir some space," he replied firmly, straightening his shoulders. My father, Haresh Oberoi, hadn't gotten where he was in life by letting people tell him what to do. As the owner of one of the most illustrious production companies in India, he knew when a firm hand was required to get things moving.

"I just want to make sure he's all settled in." My mother smoothed my hair down and gave me a forlorn look. "It's so strange, having him out of the house…"

"Well, it's for the best," I reminded her. "I'm taking care of the office down here. And it is not going to be forever. Besides, I've been here for two-and-a-half months now. I'm already settled."

"Exactly," my father agreed. "Just for six months or so, and then you can come back home again."

"Maybe steal your job, huh?" I teased him, and he chuckled.

"Trust me, these days, I wouldn't mind the break," he joked. I knew that he had worked hard his entire life to get HSR Entertainments off the ground. It wouldn't be long until he retired, and then I would be expected to step up to take over the company. That was what this trip to Delhi was about – a chance for me to prove myself by running the office out here, and confirm to him that I was able to take control of the entire company when he was ready to step back.

"You will keep in touch, won't you?" My mother seemed nervous about leaving me here all by myself. "And call Rashi, will you?"

"Sushma," my father took my mother's hand. "He's going to be fine. He's a grown man; he can take care of himself."

"Rashi knows many suitable girls and she can set him up. I know he can take care of himself, but I'm sure a grown woman wouldn't hurt," she remarked. I opened my mouth to say something, but thought better of it. I was wise enough to know that taking my mother on in issues of my singularity was only going to end in an argument. This had been a pleasant visit so far, and I didn't want to undo that.

"Anyway, you should be going," I hustled them towards the door. "Don't want to miss your flight back to Chandigarh, do you?"

With a flurry of goodbyes, they were out the door, and I was finally alone once more.

My cook, Kamlesh, had just left the villa and I could smell the delicious spices of the food she'd made for me filling the living room. I was glad to be on my own again.

I was meeting with my little sister, Rashi, the next day for lunch, but for the time being, I could just relax. My phone buzzed in my pocket before I'd so much as made it to the couch. I pulled it out and answered the call.

"Kabir, where are you right now?"

As soon as I heard my sister's frantic voice down the line, all my senses were on high alert. I wanted to drop down on my couch for the rest of the evening, but her voice erased every trace of tiredness from my body.

"Rashi? What's wrong?"

"Just… just tell me where you are right now?" she asked me again, inhaling a long breath and letting it out in a rush of static down the line.

"I'm home, at the villa," I replied. It wasn't like I was spending a whole lot of time at the club or whisking women out for dinner at fancy restaurants. You were more likely to find me with my feet propped up on the coffee table, scouring social media to see what was hot in the video world. I always liked to be ahead of the game when it came to our business, and production was one of those industries that were always changing, always evolving.

"Any of your guest rooms set up properly?" She demanded urgently.

"Yeah, I guess so," I replied hesitantly. It was an unusual question. If she wanted to stay with me for a few days, her own room was ready and well-maintained. I got to my feet and walked around the house. The villa I was living in was pretty spacious, with two floors and six bedrooms. It had a big massive living room, an open modular kitchen and was surrounded by a big garden. I knew it was a bit much for a bachelor like me to live alone, but well, my parents insisted I stayed here, and it was much easier to abide than argue.

"Why?" I asked. "Are you going to tell me what's going on?"

"Mom and dad are already gone, right?" She confirmed quickly.

"Yes, they left some time ago. They had a flight to catch," I replied, and she suddenly exhaled in relief.

"You're going to have to bear with me here, Kabir," she replied grimly. "This is going to be a lot."

"Rashi, you're worrying me," I told her, as I paced up and down the living room and kitchen.

"We carried out a raid this evening, with the cops," she explained as quickly as she could, "At a brothel on the other side of the city. Kabir, it was so much worse than we had expected…"

Her voice had started to tremble, and she stopped herself before she could get too upset, but I could hear the stress of the evening thus far written all over her tone. I closed my eyes and pinched the bridge of my nose. I just needed her to calm down and tell me what she needed from me, but whatever happened, it had clearly been enough to seriously shake her up. Which was saying something, given that she tended to get herself wrapped up in these kinds of messes all the time.

"There were so many more girls than the shelter has room for," she explained, once she had gathered herself. "We've managed to place a few of them in other places around the city, but we're running short of rooms. Could I drop one of them off with you?"

I opened my mouth to protest, but before I could say anything, she jumped in, as though sensing my resistance and needing me to give in to her.

"It would just be for a couple of days," she pleaded. "Kabir, if you'd seen what it was like in this place, you wouldn't even think twice. It was… it was bad. These women, they've spent their whole lives being exploited. I'm just asking you to put one of them up for a day or two until she can get back on her feet. Please."

I pressed my lips together and tried to talk myself out of my own selfishness. I liked to keep my space to myself. And the thought of some woman, who was in the midst of an emotional crisis after my sister had retrieved her from one of the worst things she could possibly have been wrapped up in, exhausted me just to think of it. But Rashi was right. If it were just for a couple of nights. I would have been an awful person to say no; a happier, calmer person, sure, but an awful one. Besides, if my little sister needed me, then I had to step up and do what was right. That was Big Brother 101.

"Fine, I'll do it," I agreed. "How far away are you guys now?"

"Oh, thank god," she breathed a sigh of relief. "We're nearby. I wouldn't have called you, but there were no other places I could think of, and you're so close—"

"Rashi, you've convinced me," I cut her off fondly. "You don't have to sell this idea anymore, I promise. Bring her here."

"Thank you, so much," she gushed once more. "You have no idea what you're doing here, really. You're making such a difference."

"Right, okay," I nodded. "I'll meet you outside the villa in twenty minutes? Give me time to get the guest room ready."

"Of course," she agreed, and she hesitated for a moment before she spoke again. I knew her well enough to guess that there was something else she thought I should know, but she wasn't sure if it would help or hinder what was going on.

"Rashi?" I prompted her. "What's going on?"

"Nothing, sorry. I'll bring her right over," she replied quickly. "See you soon, brother."

"See you."

She hung up the phone, and I stared at the blank screen – it was the latest model, given to me by one of the technology executives who was trying to convince us to pick their company for our latest video series. It seemed so silly now, given the seriousness of what was happening. If I'd sold this phone, how many rooms in that shelter of Rashi's could I have paid for? How many raids like the one tonight she could have pulled off?

I walked around the house and wondered which room would suit best for my guest-to-be? I crossed off my parents and Rashi's room. God forbid if my mother found out about who slept in her bed! I then scanned the guest rooms. I had three, but two were on the first floor. The third guest bedroom was relatively small, but it was right next to my own room. I decided to give it to my guest. Yes, she would feel lonely and probably scared all alone on the first floor. And given the room was right next to mine, I could cater to all her needs immediately.

I peeked inside the room. It was a small spare bedroom that led off my living room, with a single bed and a lamp perched on a tiny cabinet beside it. I wasn't even sure when last the sheets were changed in it. I knew it wasn't much, but it would do at a pinch.

I went about changing the sheet. I wasn't much used to carrying out household chores, having hired a cleaner, Seema, to keep this place spic and span since I'd moved in. But I did what I could, figuring that anything was going to be better than wherever this woman had just come from. I even lit a candle that I dug out from the back of a cupboard in the hopes of making the place more homely and to make it feel cosy. There was something churning in the pit of my stomach, and I couldn't quite put my finger on what it was. My head was thrumming with the reality of what was happening, and I had to talk myself out of calling

Rashi and making up some story about being out of town the next couple of days and just hopping in a hotel while this woman took my villa. The thought of living with an escort… it wasn't that I thought they were terrible people or anything – no, those were the attitudes my parents held, muttering about broken women and ruined virtue – but what kind of person could do that for a living? And did I want them hanging around my house for the next few days?

I pushed those thoughts to the back of my head; if Rashi was involved in this, there was a good chance that this woman hadn't exactly made the choice to take on this profession herself. Rashi, the progressive feminist campaigner in our family whose very existence and choice of career path, seemed set to annoy the older members of our family, who just wanted her to settle down and have children already, got involved in cases like this all the time. She had used the money from her inheritance to fund the operations of a shelter for women fleeing from abuse; some of them were wives leaving husbands who knocked them around, others escaping families who wanted to force them into marriages that terrified them. But most were prostitutes and escorts; women who had been trafficked into the industry and knew nothing more than prostrating their bodies in front of men who treated them like objects to be owned and used as they saw fit.

Sometimes, I wondered if I should have done something worthier with my money and my time, the way Rashi had dedicated herself. But if it hadn't been for someone like me carrying on the family business, she wouldn't have had the funds to continue doing what she was doing. I worked so she could change the world – or at least, that's what I'd told myself. I could have turned down the management position here in Delhi when my father had offered it to me, signed it off to one of our senior executives and taken some time away, but I had chosen to take it on myself, not trusting anyone but myself with the running of this place. I wanted to make sure that whenever Rashi did settle down and have kids, there was an illustrious business to support all of them, no matter what happened.

Not that I could see her settling down any time soon. That was something we did have in common. I was about as far from getting married as I could possibly be, despite the pressure both my mother and my father were applying in getting me to marry basically any woman with a finger to hold a ring. Every time I went home, they seemed to have someone else picked out for me, an appropriate but profoundly uninteresting woman they hoped that I would fall in love with on the spot and propose to already. I got it, they wanted grandchildren, but they had raised two children in whom they had fostered fierce independence and curiosity about the world. Rashi and I, we had bigger ideas than what happened in the bounds of family tradition, and our parents only had themselves to blame for that.

But sometimes I wondered if there really was something in settling down and getting married. I mean, I had been single for more than two years now, and sometimes I found myself wondering if it would have been nice to come home after a long day on the job to be met with a smile and a kiss and dinner on the table that wasn't made by Kamlesh. Maybe even with a couple of kids running around, kids I could read to and play football with on the street outside like I had done when I was a child and my dad was in a late meeting in the office. Or maybe I would move out to the country like my parents had, raise kids where I could take them on walks through the woods and show them the gorgeous heritage the place had to offer.

But either way, that was hardly going to happen any time soon. For now, I had to stay focused on what Rashi needed from me. I found myself getting nervous again. I headed to the bathroom to brush my hair and shave; I wasn't sure why I was bothering, but I wanted to look nice. I wanted to at least look respectable, given that this woman was going to be living with me for the foreseeable future. I headed downstairs to meet Rashi, crossing my arms and drumming my fingers agitatedly on my elbow as I waited. I glanced at my watch, counting down the minutes until they were due to get here. How long had she said she would be? I thought she said twenty minutes, but it had been nearly half an hour, and there was still no sign of them. A few people gave me strange looks as they passed by me on the street, as though I might have been curb-crawling, looking for a woman of the night to show me a good time. I supposed I was meeting an escort, so they weren't totally wrong... even if it wasn't exactly in the way most of them seemed to think.

I promised myself I would give it five more minutes and then I would head back inside and call Rashi again, but just as that thought crossed my mind, a car screeched around the corner and came to a sudden halt in front of me. I recognized it as Rashi's, a beaten-up old thing that she'd had since she was a teenager. How many times had I offered to get her something more modern, something that didn't look like it wasn't going to be able to take her to the end of the street? But she had always told me she was way too busy to bother picking up anything else, and I believed her. She always seemed to be up to her armpits in something that took up all of her time. I supposed we were alike in that way, both of us always mired intently in something big, whether it was the family business or a crusade to keep the women of Delhi safe.

Rashi climbed out of the car, and she came up to me before she brought the woman out. The windows were so grubby that I could barely see her, but I could make out the shape of her through the glass, could see that she was hunched over like she was trying to vanish deep inside herself.

"Kabir," Rashi gave me a quick hug, and I knew this had to be serious; like me, Rashi had never been much of a hugger. "Sorry we were late. She had a panic attack when I took her past one of the old brothels she used to work at, and I had to take a detour…"

"What do you need me to do?" I asked her, the stir of nerves picking up in my stomach once again. *Too late to back out now.* A panic attack? What if she had another one when she was with me? I had no idea how I was supposed to deal with that.

"I just need you to get her something to eat and put her in bed," Rashi instructed. She had dark rings under her eyes, but I knew she wouldn't be getting much sleep tonight. She would spend the rest of the evening making sure the rest of the women, who'd been rescued in this bust, were situated comfortably first, as well as helping the cops put together a decent report on what had happened. She'd probably make it to bed just as I would be getting up to breakfast. I had no idea how she did it.

"What do I need to know?" I asked, eyeing the woman through the window once more. I still couldn't make out much.

"Her name is Aamna," Rashi replied hurriedly, glancing at her watch. "She's been in this business for about four years. She's really not doing so well, but I think she's just going to need a decent amount of sleep in a safe place and it'll do her a world of good."

"What do I do if she has a panic attack again?" I asked nervously. I had never dealt with anything like that before. I had no idea how to relate to this woman or how to handle her if she freaked out on me.

"Honestly, she's exhausted," Rashi yawned. "She'll pass out as soon as you get her to bed. And I'll come around again soon to help out, okay?"

"Okay," I sighed, and she wrapped her arms around me once more.

"You're a good man, Kabir," she murmured in my ear. "Better than you know."

She swiftly extracted herself from me and went to let Aamna out of the car. I tried her name out in my head a couple of times. *Aamna, Aamna, Aamna.* It sounded familiar somehow, as though it had been on the tip of my tongue for as long as I could recall and only now I had remembered it.

Rashi opened the car door and offered Aamna a hand. I took a look at the woman. She was a little shorter than Rashi, or maybe it was just the way she was holding herself; shoulders hunched, head tilted down, arms wrapped tightly around herself as though she wanted nothing more than to disappear on the spot. She was wearing a large men's t-shirt and a pair of leggings that had clearly been given to her as part of the raid, just to cover herself up. The clothes were enormous on her and hung off her willowy frame, making her look even tinier. She had a curtain of long, dark hair that ran down to her waist, unkempt and messy, and her skin was the colour of the fresh bark of a sapling.

She flicked her gaze up to meet mine, and my heart lurched in my chest when I looked into her eyes for the first time – she had pale eyes, grey-green, glinting in the streetlights above us. She looked wary, as though she was an animal caught in the headlights of an oncoming car and about to dart back into the safety of the black forest.

I wasn't sure exactly what I felt when I looked at her for the first time; pity, of course, and sadness at whatever had happened that had made this woman so apparently determined to vanish deep inside herself. But more than anything, I wanted to take her into my arms and tell her that it was going to be alright. I had no idea if that was true, but I felt this swell of certainty, and in that moment, I truly believed that I could take care of her, could protect her, and could make it all better.

"Aamna, this is my brother, Kabir," Rashi explained to her slowly, taking her elbow to guide her towards me. Aamna hadn't taken her eyes off of me, as though she expected me to lunge at her if she looked away even for a split second. Aamna nodded slowly, and I offered her a smile. I noticed, all at once, that there were tears streaking down her face, make-up smudged beneath her eyes. I wondered if it was the rescue that had brought her to tears or something that had happened before my sister had gotten to her. The thought of someone hurting her, of reducing her to this state, made my blood boil in my veins.

"You're going to be staying with him for a little while, alright?" Rashi explained. "I'll be back first thing tomorrow. And as soon as the shelter has a spare bed for you, we'll come and pick you up, and you can be with your friends. Okay?"

"They aren't my friends," Aamna mumbled, her voice tiny. "The women I worked with, they were just as bad as me..."

Rashi furrowed her brow, and I could tell she wanted to tell Aamna off for speaking that way about the other girls who suffered the same fate, but she knew there was no point. This was a woman who had been through enough for one evening. Why push things any further?

"Kabir has a spare bed for you upstairs," Rashi told her. "I have to go now, but Kabir has my number and of the shelter, if you need to call me for anything, alright?"

Aamna nodded, falling mute once more. Rashi glanced at me and looked pointedly to the woman standing next to her, indicating that I should come over and take her from there. I stepped towards her and waited for her to move, but she didn't. She was staring blankly into the space, wondering what to do. I felt I needed to encourage her. Hence, I gingerly placed a hand on the small of her back; though she flinched, she didn't pull away. Even though it was a warm night, she was shaking and trembling. "Take this," Rashi grabbed a bag from the back of the car and handed it to me. "It has everything she'll need – clothes, toiletries. I'll see you soon, alright? I've got to go take care of things at the shelter."

And with that, my sister left me in the middle of the night with a woman I had never so much as laid eyes on before, a woman who clearly needed my help. I guided Aamna towards the door, and she hung back as I unlocked it and pushed it open.

"You want to come in?" I asked, and she stood there for a moment, chewing her lip so hard that I was surprised that it didn't draw blood. Eventually, after a long pause, she scurried inside and glanced over her shoulder at me, eyes wide, as though she expected me to do something to her, now that I had her all by herself.

"Hey, you're alright." I soothed her, holding my hands up to show that I had no intention of hurting her. "You want something to eat? You must be hungry."

She paused for another moment, like she didn't want to admit to needing anything from me, and then she nodded.

"Yes, I'm starving." She pressed her closed fist into her stomach like she was angry at herself for requiring my help.

"Here, take this!" I handed her the bag Rashi had given me. I quickly walked towards the door of her room and opened it wide for her. "This would be your room. And the bathroom is right there. You get yourself cleaned up, okay? My cook has prepared some snacks; I'll heat them up for you…"

She darted away from me before I could finish what I was saying, and I watched as she closed the door tight behind her and drew the bolt across, the metal scraping on the wood. I couldn't help but wonder what she had been through to make her this nervous around me, but there was no point delving into that now – she would be gone in a few days, and I didn't want to get too invested in her.

I turned to the kitchen to fix us some food; it had been a hell of a long day for me, and I was hungry too. I laid out some food on a couple of plates – some *samosas*, some rice, and a few *pakoras* – and put them carefully on the coffee table in the living room. I could hear the water running in the bathroom, and I wondered if I should go and check on her, but the last thing she probably needed was me startling her by a sudden knock or barging in and invading her privacy when she had only just gotten out of that awful place.

Eventually, she emerged once more; her hair was pulled back, and her face was scrubbed clean. She looked far younger than she had when she had stepped out of that car a few minutes before. Her arms were dangling by her sides, and she was still wearing those enormous clothes, like she was hiding inside them, trying to make herself invisible.

"Here," I pointed to the plates on the table. "Have something to eat. My sister will kill me if you don't, so you owe me."

The barest flicker of a smile passed across her face. She still had that feeling around her, as though she was a wild animal about to flee; it was clear that whatever she had been through, it had affected her profoundly, deep down to the depths of her soul. As she perched on the edge of the couch next to me, she stole a look at me and then picked up the plate.

"Thank you," she muttered, and she began to tuck into the food like she had never seen it before in her life. She ate quickly, as though she half-expected me to lean over and swipe the food from her the first chance I got. I looked away and focused on my own meal. I had been at work all day, and I had a habit of forgetting to eat when I was really busy. Maybe having her around, having to feed her and make sure that she got enough rest, would force me to do the same for myself.

I wanted to talk to her, but I had no idea what I could speak to her about. The usual small-talk subjects were off the table – I could hardly ask her how she'd found the weather lately, or where she was from originally, when the fact of her past was burning, unspoken, between us. But I didn't want to delve into that, either. The last thing I needed was to send her off into another spiral of panic and fear that I might not be able to handle as well as Rashi.

She finished her food quickly, and then leaned back in the seat and closed her eyes; for a moment, she actually looked relaxed, at peace, like any other young woman finishing up a particularly hard day. How old was she? I had no idea, but Rashi had said she'd been stuck in that hell-hole for the last four years, so she couldn't have been much more than a teenager when she got trafficked into it.

"Would you like more?" I asked, and she shook her head.

"No, that was fine," she replied, and she offered me a shy smile. "Thank you."

"You're welcome," I smiled back, and just like that I felt as though something had shifted between us; we had shared a meal together. Would this be a tantamount to a first date, in a funny twisted-up kind of way. Well, I would take that for now.

"What else do you need?" I asked. "Rashi said there was everything in that bag, but if there's something else—"

"I have everything," she replied, blinking at me a couple of times. "I think I'm going to go to bed now."

"Okay," I got to my feet. "Here, let me show you to your room. Earlier when she had come out of the bathroom, I was so hung up at her cleaned look that I hadn't even noticed that she had carried her bag with her. Slowly, she picked up her bag full of necessities and followed me, yawning quietly as she went. As she got up, I noticed that she was wearing a thin anklet around her leg; delicate and silver, which jingled a little as she walked. I stared at it for a short moment, the movement of the anklet entrancing me.

She was near-silent, so much so that I could have forgotten that she was there entirely – was that how she'd been taught to act all this time? Seen and not heard? The thought filled me with anger, an anger that I couldn't articulate. I just wanted to protect her and to prove to her that nobody would dare treat her like that as long as I was around.

"Goodnight," she murmured to me, and she looked up at me once more. As soon as my gaze met hers, met those grey-green eyes that seemed to gleam like gems in the half-light of the street outside, I felt my heart jolt once more. She was exceptionally beautiful, like someone had gone out of their way to craft something perfect – only to break it down, to force her into the profession that would make her doubt her beauty and everything else about herself.

"Goodnight, Aamna," I replied, and I pulled the door shut behind me and let out a long breath I didn't know I'd been holding. I went to the living room and cleaned up the plates, hoping they would be enough to draw my mind away from the starkness of the image of her eyes burning in my brain. There was a familiarity there, somehow, just like there had been when I heard her name for the first time. Like something had slotted into place.

I pushed those thoughts to the back of my mind and went to bed. I would take the day off work the next day so I could be there when Rashi arrived, and so I could at least make sure that Aamna was doing okay. I knew that I should feel indifferent, that having Aamna in my house shouldn't affect me, but I wasn't like Rashi, I didn't engage with these kinds of women all the time, and I rarely got to see that kind of pain and trauma written close-up on the faces of the people who had suffered it. It was only natural that I should want to care for her. And I was going to indulge that natural instinct for as long as it took for her to get back on her feet.

I lay in bed that night and stared at the ceiling. It took me longer than usual to get to sleep, the image of the woman in the bedroom next to me going round and round my head until it felt as though it had been there forever. When my eyes drifted shut and sleep took me, I found myself dreaming of a grey-green gaze that felt as though it was setting my mind on fire.

2

Aamna

I lay in bed and stared at the ceiling, listening to the sounds of the street below, and tried to put myself to sleep. But it didn't work. The adrenalin was still pulsing around my body, and everything in me was telling me that I should still be terrified that they were coming back to get me.

I still didn't really know how I'd ended up in this place. I lifted my head and looked around the room; it was small but well-appointed, like whoever owned this place had money to spare. I hadn't slept anywhere but on that bare mattress on that rusted bed frame in the room that had been my prison for so long that it had started to feel like home.

The man – Kabir? That woman had told me his name, but my brain had been in flight mode, and I had been unable to take in anything significant. The man who owned this place, he had given me food and had tried to speak to me, but all I had been able to do was stare back at him and wait for him to stop. I didn't know how to talk to men. I knew how to – I knew how to read them, to give them what they wanted with my body. But when it came to actually speak to them, to someone who wasn't trying to use me and dispose of me, I had no idea how that worked.

It felt like the life I'd had before I was taken was a million miles away. In reality, it was only a few years, but everything about me had changed beyond recognition. All that I had been was corrupted now, all that hope and excitement for the future warped and ruined and turned into a bad dream of servitude and man after man after man after man.

How many times had I gone back in my head, and prayed for a chance not to apply for the modelling job that had brought me there? I had seen it advertised in the salon one of my aunties had taken me to, someone looking for hair models to shoot for their salon, and she had nudged me towards giving it a go.

"What have you got to lose?" she asked, stroking my hair. "You're so beautiful. You should be on a billboard somewhere!"

"I don't think it's going to be a billboard, aunty," I laughed, and she grinned and shrugged. I could still remember exactly how that conversation had gone, the moment when my life had changed forever. I had willed myself, with every fibre in my body, to go back to that moment, not to notice the advertisement, for my aunty to not encourage me to go for it, to chicken out and focus on where I wanted to go to college. But nothing, not even my deepest, hardest attempts, pulled me back to the start. However, every time I opened my eyes, I always found myself in that place again, the walls creeping with rising damp, the same kind that felt as though it was inching up and corrupting my soul.

I had called the number on the advertisement, and they had invited me in for an audition. I had deliberately neglected to mention it to my parents, worried they would think I was vain or silly. Maybe if I had told them where I was going that day, when I had skipped out the door carefully made-up and feeling pretty, someone would have come to break me out sooner. Or maybe that was just wishful thinking, and they would have just convinced my family that they were wrong and I must have run away.

By the time I arrived at the interview, I was starting to sense something was off. It was taking place at the Benito Juarez Marg, a part of the city that my mother would have raised her eyebrows at.

My heart always gave a jolt and sank every time I thought about my mother. I don't remember since when, but I had lost track of time in that hell-hole. It felt like a lifetime, as though I had lived a whole existence separate from her. An era since we had last seen one another. That hurt, more than I ever would have cared to admit. I could have seen her again, both my parents, if I wanted – but the thought of looking into their eyes and telling them the truth of what had happened to me was far too painful to consider. I couldn't let them see what I had become. I couldn't hurt them that way, with the truth. What if they thought less of me? What if they never saw me the same way again? What if they saw me as an impossible broken creature, so far removed from their daughter that they no longer knew me? Panic flooded through me again. I couldn't tell them. Not yet. Not even when I was free now…

But, despite what my mother might have said, I had convinced myself that attending the audition was fine – it was the middle of the day, the place would be jam-packed, and there would be plenty of other girls at the audition with me. We would be able to keep each other safe. I should have trusted my gut instinct and run in the other direction.

The auditions were being held in a warehouse, and I once again soothed my worries, convincing myself that it was just because they needed to get a whole lighting rig in there to shoot the pictures. However, as soon as I stepped through the door, everything changed.

The warehouse was enormous and nearly-empty, as though it hadn't been used in years; there were maybe a half-dozen men, most of them older than me, except for one who looked terrified and as though he was barely sixteen. The door slid shut behind me with a loud clang that filled my head and rang in my ears. I wanted nothing more than to dive back out onto the safety of the street. But I stood there, frozen to the spot, feeling as though my feet had been rooted to the ground. Why couldn't I just run out of there? There was so obviously something wrong and yet I was just standing there like I was afraid of being rude to these men who clearly meant me harm. My mind flickered back to those news stories I'd seen, the ones about women being gang-raped by groups of men, and my pulse began to race.

One of them, the one I would later come to know as Shekhar, stepped forward. His mouth was set in a hard line, and his eyes swept over my body, up and down, taking me in and judging me on the spot.

"Aamna?"

I nodded. I couldn't speak. My tongue felt as though it had swollen in my mouth, useless, dumb. The man, Shekhar, glanced to the men on either side of him and nodded, and they stepped forward; one of them pulled a black fabric bag over my head, and the other secured my arms behind my back, and that's when I finally started to fight.

"No!" I screamed at the top of my lungs. The man was gripping my wrists so tight it felt like he was going to punch through my skin. I tried to wrench myself away from him, but even if I managed to pull away from him, there were so many others ready to jump in and take his place. I couldn't get away. They had gotten me. For whatever they wanted me for, they had gotten me. The panic swelled and took over, and my legs trembled out from beneath me as I passed out from the fear.

By the time I woke, I was not in the warehouse, but in a place where even my worst nightmares hadn't ever taken me. In fact, it took me a week to find out where I was. I was certain that they had whisked me across the country, far from anyone who could have found me, but later I realized that they had moved me just a few miles from my home.

Shekhar was the one who came into that pathetic little room and told me my place in all of this. I wrapped the covers around me as I wriggled away from him, knowing what my fate was, but reluctant to accept it. He sat down on the edge of my bed – the way my father had done when I was a child to read me stories – and he touched my leg in an attempt to soothe me. I whipped it away from him at once. I couldn't stand his touch on me, couldn't stand anything about him. He had dark hair streaked with blonde highlights and an earring that glittered dully in the light. His eyes were dark, with a cruelty to them that I had never seen in anyone before. I had met mean people, sure, but the way he looked at me – it was as though he didn't even see me as a person. It was like he had stripped me of my humanity with a single glance. I hated it, hated the way it made me feel.

"You work for me now," he told me simply. "You sleep with who I send in here, and I take your earnings. If you try to get away, I'll kill your family. I know where they live. Not far from here, right?"

I stared at him. He could have just been bluffing, of course – it was a fair guess, given that I had come to the audition in this city, and that my family lived here, but I would never call him on that bluff. I would never dare.

"Do you understand?" He tapped my leg, and I knew he was communicating with me that my body was no longer my own. If he wanted to, he could have done anything he wanted to do. Yes, today it was just a touch, but tomorrow it could be anything, if I

didn't do as I was told. I wanted to scream. I wanted to tear my hair out. I wanted to fight him, to escape this place and flee back to my family. I looked down at my feet and realized they had taken my shoes away, as though they had no intention for me to step outside ever again.

The terror that I felt that day never really went away. It just transformed into something more muted, so I could get through every day in that place. I counted each and every one. The days seemed to spread out in front of me fearfully, blurring together. One man, two men, three men, more. I was a virgin when they took me to that place, but that soon changed. I knew they would come up again at some point, which I would have to face up to the long nightmare I had lived out for all those months.

Shekhar was the worst part of it. I was pretty sure he saw me as something more than just an earner for him. The other girls – not that I was allowed to see them much – they just made cash for him. He abused and exploited them, but he rarely laid a finger on them himself. But with me, it was different. At least, that's what he told me. He would slide into that bed next to me and touch me, hold me and do vile things while I lay there, stiff as a board, waiting for it all to be over. I couldn't believe that he really thought there was something to the two of us, that he couldn't understand that I would lay there and pretend that I was somewhere, anywhere else in the world. He told me he loved me a few times, and I wouldn't reply, hoping to god that it would be over soon. After one of his clients broke into my room one evening and slept with me without paying, he installed a lock on the inside of the door, and as much as I could, I would make sure it was firmly bolted over, so I didn't have to deal with his sick advances.

I had heard whispers before they came for us. Shekhar was more stressed than usual; I knew because he came to see me more often. He wouldn't say anything to my face, but I would press my ear to the door and listen to the hushed voices outside, to mention of the police and other people inching closer to us. But I didn't put any stock in it. Why would I? Nobody had come looking for me, nobody had found me, and nobody would save me. This was my life, for as long as I was forced to live it, and I had to accept that.

So, when they came for me, I didn't believe it at first. That woman Rashi, the one who had brought me here, she had been the one to open the door and walk in to find me. When I laid my eyes on her, I instantly wanted to dive beneath the covers. Men had exploited me and used me all this time, but I wasn't sure how I should handle a woman. She reached out her hand to me, and suddenly my ear tuned in to commotion outside, and I realized something was happening, something big.

"I'm Rashi," she spoke gently. She had kind eyes and a gentle demeanour, but it had been so long since someone had come to me with anything other than a total disregard for my being that it took me a moment to realize what she was doing.

"What are you doing here?" I demanded, and she offered me a smile.

"I'm getting you out of here," she told me. "I know it's hard, but you have to come with me. I'm here with the police, and we don't know how long we've got before the people who run this place come back with back-up. The rest of the girls are outside. We have room in the shelter for all of you. Okay?"

"No," I shook my head. I didn't believe her. I couldn't handle this; the promise of freedom that I knew was going to be whipped away from me at a moment's notice.

"I know this is hard for you to believe," Rashi repeated, patient but urgent. "But if you come with us now, we can keep you safe. I promise. Please, we want to get you out of here."

I stared at her for a long time, and then slowly swung my feet out of the bed; I half-expected alarms to go off as soon as they hit the floor, but nothing happened. Rashi beckoned me towards her with her hand and I stood up and moved towards her. I brushed by her to the door and peered outside; there was a small huddle out there, of most of the girls that I'd seen working here over the years. It hit me then, or at least began to, that this was actually happening.

It all came in a rush after that. They had rescued so many girls tonight that the shelter ran out of place. They had started putting us all up at various locations, and that's when the woman who had found me, Rashi, had made that frantic phone call and then driven me across the city. After the rescue, I had stood there outside the shelter, staring at the night sky above me; even though I couldn't see the stars, thanks to the city lights blurring them, I couldn't help but hook into the impossible expanse of it, the freedom. I breathed in the air, and it tasted fresh, new. It still hadn't really sunk in, and I kept waiting for the rug to whip out from underneath me. Every time I blinked, I expected to open my eyes and find myself back in that place once more. The image of it, of all that had happened to me in there, was burned onto the back of my brain, branded there.

"We can take you to your parents, if you want," Rashi suggested softly, gently touching my hand. "Do you want me to take you there?"

A horrifying shock jolted through my spine. I shook my head at once. No way that I could let them see all of this. Everything and everyone I was carrying with me. The thought of it spiked through my system, barbed at the edges. No, I couldn't do this to them. "Alright," Rashi replied, furrowing her brow. "Give me a minute..." and she had made that frantic phone call.

After a phone call, she ushered me into her car, and I slid into the back seat.

"The man I'm taking you to stay with is my brother," Rashi had told me in the car, hurriedly catching me up. I stared out of the window. The streets running by us felt impossibly new, as though I had never set foot in the city before. I was twenty years old and felt as though I had just been born, like I had just dropped out of the sky.

"His name is Kabir, and he'll be able to take care of you," she continued. "I'm sorry we don't have room for you in the shelter right now, but we will soon, very soon. And then we'll be able to see about getting you into therapy, alright? To help you deal with everything."

"Sure," I muttered. I could hardly think. My brain was overfull and yet completely blank at the same time, and as she pulled the car to a halt and introduced me to her brother, I felt like I was wafting through a trance.

Her brother, Kabir, he is handsome. It was the kind of name that my mother would have nodded approvingly at, the old-fashioned sort that suited a man of his standing. He was clearly not expecting guests that evening, but he was clean-shaven and smelled good, like an expensive aftershave. His eyes were dark but kind, just like his sister's. And when he touched his hand lightly to my back as he guided me, I found myself relaxing. It was the strangest feeling. For the longest time, I had associated a man's touch with pain, with cruelty, and with all the unspeakable violations that I had suffered. Knowing that he wasn't going to do that to me, was novel – although there was nothing he could do to come close to the pain that those men had inflicted on me. His presence was relieving.

He fed me and put me to bed, and I lay awake and listened to him go to his own room. There was a part of me that wanted to go to him, to slide beneath the covers next to him, to feel his warm body next to mine.

But maybe I shouldn't be so quick to trust him. Men, after all, had been the ones to put me where I had been for the last four years – they had been the ones who had used me, not caring for the agony written all over my face as they did what they wanted with me. Perhaps what I had seen these last few years was the truth inside all men, the parts that they hid from their wives and children and the people who loved them. How many men had come into that room with wedding rings, or the tan lines where they had slid them off? How many of their wives knew what they were doing, the kind of people they really were? The monstrousness that hid inside them, inside all the men who used women like me, maybe it was in all of them. Maybe I shouldn't trust a single one.

I stared at the ceiling and found myself wondering if perhaps I had found one who was different. Maybe I could just cling to that hope for now. Maybe, if I had any hope of making it out of this with my sanity, with myself intact, I had to start believing in the good in people once more. And believing in the good of the man who had taken me in was a decent place to start.

I closed my eyes and drifted off to sleep, and found myself resting soundly for what felt like the first time in my entire life.

3

Kabir

"Hey, Kabir, I'm on my way over," Rashi yawned down the line, as I swallowed the first bite of the breakfast. The whole morning, my phone had been pinned between my shoulder and my ear. I had already called into work to tell them I wouldn't be in that day. I had asked my secretary to rearrange all of my meetings so that none of my clients were unhappy. And I had also checked in on the status of the today's shoot. I was supposed to stay home with Aamna, but the work at HSR Entertainments must go on. Spending my time with Aamna was not a requirement Rashi had stated, it was I who didn't want to leave Aamna all by herself in the villa. She had seemed so jumpy and nervous the day before, the last thing she needed was to find herself alone in an unfamiliar place.

"Oh, okay." I got to my feet and started pacing. "You want to see Aamna?"

"Yeah, I need to talk to her about a few things," she replied. "See if she's willing to talk to the police and help the investigation against the men who exploited her."

"You really think that's a good idea so soon after you got her out?" I wondered aloud. I glanced towards the closed door of the guest room, where Aamna was presumably still sleeping. I had heard her get up to go to the bathroom during the night, and I thought I heard her crying. I had considered going through and seeing if she was alright, but I had no idea what to say to her.

"Honestly, no, but we need to move fast if we're going to gather all the evidences we need." She sighed. "If I had it my way, they could take some time to get counselling before they had to deal with anything too intense, but the sooner they reveal all the vital information, the better chance we will have of conducting a successful prosecution."

"Christ, I didn't realize how much went into an investigation like this," I muttered, pinching the bridge of my nose. It hurt to think that there were more girls like Aamna, a whole bunch of them, who were probably suffering the same way she was. If I could have gotten my hands on the men who had done this…

"Yeah, well, the sooner I can get this over with, the better." Rashi sighed. "I'll be there in about half an hour, okay?"

"Okay," I replied. "I'll make sure she's up."

"Thanks, brother," Rashi replied, and she hung up the phone and left me in silence once more. I looked down at the food in front of me and suddenly wasn't hungry anymore. The thought of what she must be going through made me a little sick.

Suddenly, the door to Aamna's room opened, and I glanced up to see her standing there, I averted my gaze at once, but before I could, it was impossible not to notice how long and slender her limbs looked under that enormous shirt.

"Hey!" I greeted her. I felt stupid as I greeted a pillar next to her. I looked back at her and focused only on her face, and not on her bare legs. "Did you sleep well?" I asked.

She nodded, and her eyes were drawn to the food on the table in front of me.

"You want something to eat?" I questioned.

"Yes, thank you," she replied, her voice small and careful, as though she was worried that if she said the wrong thing, I would blow up at her. I wanted to soothe her, to tell her that I wasn't going to treat her the way those awful men must have, but I didn't want to draw attention to her clear discomfort. She was already distinctly aware of that.

She took her seat at the counter, tucking her legs up underneath her carefully; it seemed she was trying to make herself as small as possible. There was a little make-up smudged on her face, and her eyes flicked up to meet mine for the briefest moment as I put the plate down in front of her. She managed a smile.

"Thank you," she said again, and she began to eat. I busied myself around the kitchen just so I wasn't standing there and staring at her while she ate, but I was distinctly aware of every single one of her reactions; as one of the plates clattered against another, she jerked sharply, as though she had been struck. I fought the sudden urge to wrap my arms around her, to hold her close and protect her from everything that surrounded her, but I had to remember my boundaries. It wasn't my place. She had to come to trusting me, to trusting anyone, on her own. I couldn't force it.

She watched me as I made my way around the kitchen, and I could feel her eyes burning into me as though she was trying to see into my soul.

"Are you alright?" I asked, glancing over at her, and she lowered her eyes at once, as though she had been caught out.

"You're allowed to look at me, Aamna," I assured her, and she pushed her hand through her long hair and met my gaze once more. Though she didn't say anything, she looked me dead in the eye, and that seemed to be enough for her for now. There was sadness in her beautiful grey green eyes that pained me, a depth of agony that was unique to her. I didn't even want to think about what she had been through.

"Rashi's going to be here soon," I told her. "She needs to talk to you about… about what happened."

She winced, as though she couldn't think of anything worse.

"Do you want to get cleaned up?" I asked. "I can run you a bath."

She smiled, and it reached her eyes this time.

"I'd like that," she replied softly. "Thank you."

I got to my feet and headed through to the bathroom, where I ran her a bath; I poured in some oil, it smelled good, of Jasmine, and the scent seemed to suit her well; deep, musky, a little mysterious. I took the candle and lit it in the bathroom, and laid out a clean towel for her. Normally I would have just gotten the cleaner to do this for me, but I wanted to take care of her myself; a sensation I had never really felt before, at least for anybody outside the family.

I made my way back to the kitchen and found her staring off into space, the corners of her mouth turned down, her eyes glazed as though she was lost deep in some memory.

"Aamna?" I asked her softly. She blinked and smiled as she met my gaze.

"Yes?" she replied softly.

"Your bath is ready," I told her. She got to her feet and stretched, and the shirt rode up a few inches to show off a strip of her slim figure. I looked away again. She probably wasn't used to modesty, having come from the situation she'd come from, but I still felt like I was intruding when I looked at her like that.

She brushed by me on the way to the bathroom, and the briefest of touches was all that I needed to send an explosion of tingles over my skin. I wanted to reach out, to slide my arm around her slim waist and draw her against me, to wrap her in my arms and promise her that she would be safe. But she needed space. As the door clicked shut behind her and I heard her slip into the water with a small splash, I furrowed my brow. I didn't know where these feelings had come from. Perhaps it was as simple as the fact that I had been living like a lone wolf for a long time. There was a comfort to her company, even if I couldn't really define it, even in my own head.

I busied myself, switching on my laptop and replying to a couple of emails from work to keep myself distracted until Rashi got there. Even though I knew she was right, and that she needed to speak to Aamna if they had any hope of bringing those awful men to justice, part of me wanted to turn her away, just to give Aamna a little more space to process all that she had been through. But this was Rashi's business, not mine, and she knew far better than me.

I got absorbed in my work, and suddenly there was a knock on the door that made me jump. I had been so lost in my thoughts that I had almost forgotten Rashi was coming. "You look exhausted," I told her bluntly, and she cocked an eyebrow at me.

"Sugarcoat it for me, why don't you?" she shot back, glancing around the kitchen and living room as she strolled inside. "Where's Aamna?"

"I ran her a bath," I gestured to the bathroom. "I'm not sure how long she's going to be in there."

"Let her take all the time she needs," Rashi flopped down on the sofa and stretched. "How did she seem last night? And this morning?"

"Nervous," I replied, "And a little shocked. It doesn't seem like it's really sunk in for her yet."

"That was how she was when I came to get her," she replied. "Initially, she couldn't believe that any of it was really happening. It's probably going to take her a while to actually believe that she isn't just going to be taken back there the first chance they get."

I shook my head, a surge of anger running through me. Seeing the damage those men had caused first-hand made it all the more real, all the uglier.

"How are you doing?" I asked her, and she pulled a face.

"I feel like I'm just running on fumes right now," she admitted. "It's been so much, the last couple of days. The things that these girls have been through – I don't know how I'm meant to help them through it. It's just all so awful."

"I'm so proud of you, Rashi," I told her sincerely. "I really am. I can't think of anyone else who would do this for these women."

"There are more of us than you'd think." She smiled at me. "And people are putting up with such shit less and less. I don't think we're going to have trouble getting the cops to pay attention to us."

"Are you telling me they didn't before?" I furrowed my brow. She shrugged.

"They didn't take it as seriously as I'd have hoped in the past," she replied, and the tiredness in her voice took me by surprise. A kind of bone-deep exhaustion seemed to run deep down inside of her, in the face of all that she had seen, all that she had done, all that she had fought for.

"Then I'm even prouder of you," I replied. "You're fighting for what's right. I think I understand that better now."

I glanced towards the bathroom door, where I could hear Aamna moving around inside. Something about the sound of her soothed me. She was safe, and as long as I was around, nothing was going to happen to her.

"How are you finding having her around so far?" she asked.

"Been a while since I had a woman in the place," I remarked, and she cocked an eyebrow at me.

"Yeah, who was the last one?" She tapped her finger on her chin, as though she was pondering the question, but both she and I knew damn well who that was.

"Chhaya," I replied, and she pulled a face as soon as the word was out of my mouth.

"As if I could ever forget," she rolled her eyes. "Remind me what you saw in her, again?"

Before I could reply, Aamna emerged from the bathroom, wrapped in a towel; her eyes widened when she saw the two of us sitting there, and I swiftly averted my gaze. But not before I had noticed how long her legs looked bare, how the delicate anklet glinted just above her left foot. All scrubbed clean, with her hair pulled back into a bun, she looked younger, more vulnerable than she had before.

"Rashi," she muttered, and she glanced down at her near-nakedness. "I should – can I get dressed?"

"You don't have to ask that," Rashi assured her kindly. "Take all the time you need. I'm not going anywhere."

"Thanks," Aamna replied. Her voice was a little breathy and thin like she half-expected Rashi to tell her that she wasn't allowed to get changed. How long had she lived this way, at the command of the people who had exploited her?

She retreated into the guest bedroom, and Rashi smiled as she closed the door behind her.

"Perhaps not the greatest idea to give her a room with no attached bathroom," I muttered, cursing internally.

"Maybe, but you made the best choice. She couldn't have survived upstairs," Rashi spoke glancing around the villa. I sighed and nodded.

"She's already looking better," she continued after a brief pause. "She's going to be alright. I can feel it."

"I'll give the two of you some privacy," I suggested. If I was being honest, I didn't want to hear what Aamna had to say to Rashi. I had already heard enough about her past to date, and I wasn't sure I could handle anymore at that moment.

I headed to my bedroom, picked up my laptop and checked in on some work emails. Luckily, it was a quiet month on the job, so I didn't need to be in the office to keep an eye on things – we were between productions right now, having just wrapped on our last series; which was good news, as I didn't want to leave Aamna alone in the house, not quite yet.

Much as I tried to give the two of them their privacy, I found my ear tuning in to the conversation they were having outside. Rashi was speaking gently and softly, but Aamna was responding as though she was yelling every question at her – voice nervous, barbed, and trying to deflect. She offered one-word answers, sometimes just noises of affirmation.

Eventually, I got to my feet and stood near the door, my curiosity getting the better of me. I just wanted to hear what was going on out there. It was strange to me, having my house so full of people. I spent most of my time at work, and the most socializing I did was with clients from out of town or the odd dinner with my parents when they passed through the city. There was something about having someone so up in my personal space that made me a little uncomfortable, like she would uncover some part of me that I had been trying my best to keep from everyone around me all this time. But some other part of me – well, maybe that part of me was ready to expose myself in that fashion, to reveal the corners of my soul that I had kept shrouded in darkness all these years.

"And can you tell me what the name of the man who ran this place was?" Rashi asked. Aamna paused for a long while, and I could hear her feet shuffling against the polished wood floor below.

"Shekhar," she replied finally. The way she spoke his name was drenched in fear, as though it had soaked deep into her in a way she could never escape. The depth of her panic was palpable, even from behind the door. I felt a surge of protectiveness once more, and it caught me off-guard. I knew she needed space, but I wanted to keep her in my arms and convince her that the world would never get close to her again. That she could spend the rest of her life hidden out here, if that's what she needed.

"Okay, thank you," Rashi replied, and I heard her scribbling something down. I wondered if that was the same name the other girls had given. How far had that man's power extended? How many women had he left traumatised in his wake? I had so many questions, but the only woman who could give me those answers seemed determined to keep her mouth shut.

Rashi and Aamna exchanged a few more questions and answers, but I couldn't make out the specifics of what she was saying. I went back to my emails and tapped out a few replies on autopilot. I couldn't focus on the work in front of me. Aamna was filling my head. It would probably be better, in the grand scheme of things, if she went back to the shelter. I felt as though I wasn't going to get anything done as long as she was around. I was distracted, already a little compelled by her.

When I heard the two of them fall silent, I decided it was safe to emerge from the bedroom once more. Aamna was curled on the couch, back in the sweatpants and large t-shirt she had been wearing the night before. She lifted her gaze to look at me when I walked in, and she managed a small smile. I returned it at once, and for a moment that was the only thing in the whole world that mattered, the smile on her face, the look she gave me, as though I was her saviour.

"I think that's all I need for now," Rashi got to her feet and tucked the notebook she'd been writing in back into her bag. "Kabir, can I talk to you for a moment? In private?"

"Of course," I nodded, and I felt Aamna watching me as I led Rashi out into the hallway. Her gaze was cautious, but not as frightened as she had been the night before.

Rashi planted her hands on her hips and sighed as soon as we were alone together.

"I think she's going to have to stay here a little while longer," she told me bluntly. "We don't have room in the shelter yet, and besides, I don't think it's a good idea to move her so soon. She needs some stability for a while. Do you think you can manage that?"

I fell silent for a moment. I knew I should have just asked Rashi if Aamna could leave. I didn't want to get attached to her, not this soon into knowing her – she had been through so much, and the last thing she needed was another man swinging into her life and imposing his beliefs on her, his will. And it wasn't like I was going to get anything done as long as she was around. I could have offered to put her into a hotel, to pay for an apartment all of her own where Rashi could keep an eye on her, where she could have her privacy and safety once again.

And yet, I didn't want to say goodbye to her. It had been barely twelve hours since she had arrived in my villa, and the thought of sending her away made my stomach churn. I remembered the anklet on her leg, the delicate loop of metal that glinted up at me as she walked, and my heart leapt in my chest. I needed to keep her around. I was certain of that. "Yes, of course, she can stay," I agreed finally. Rashi closed her eyes and planted her hands together, as though thanking some god for my acceptance of the situation.

"Thank you," she reached out and squeezed my shoulder. "I know this must be hard for you, but we'll get her somewhere more permanent as soon as we can, alright?"

"There's really no rush," I assured her, surprising myself. "She can stay as long as she needs to."

"You're doing a good thing, Kabir," Rashi went to head back to the living room. "She needs someone like you, someone who can actually make her believe that not all men are total trash."

"I'll do my best." I laughed. "Glad you have so much faith in me."

Rashi opened the door and went over to Aamna, who was watching the two of us nervously from where she was sitting. I couldn't help but notice, once again, how small she looked in those enormous clothes.

"If it's alright with you, Aamna, I want you to stay here a little longer," Rashi told her. She reached out to pat Aamna on the shoulder as she passed, and Aamna jumped a little, as though the touch had sent an electric shock through her. She flushed slightly, embarrassed.

"That's okay," Aamna agreed. I smiled at her.

"I'm happy to have you here as long as you want," I told her, emphatic.

"Thank you," Aamna stared up at me again, those pale grey-green eyes wide and almost shockingly beautiful. I opened and closed my mouth, intending to come out with something clever and failing dismally.

"Okay, I'm going to leave you guys to it," Rashi headed for the door. "And actually get some sleep. You need anything – either of you – you call me, alright? I'm here for both of you."

"Will do," I hugged her goodbye, and murmured in her ear. "You take care of yourself. I've got this."

"I know you do, brother," she murmured back, and she pulled away and shot a wave at Aamna. "I'll be back to see you soon, okay?"

"Okay," Aamna nodded, and as soon as Rashi stepped out the door, she seemed to relax. Suddenly, I was distinctly aware of how alone the two of us were. I made my way back over to the couch and sat on the seat next to her; she smelled sweet from the bath, but there was something underlying that, the deep, musky, mysterious scent of Aamna. Aamna, and all the promises she held. Aamna, and all the secrets I might never know. I felt her energy, her essence, coming off her in waves, and I could already feel it beginning to imprint on me in a way that nobody else ever had before.

4

Aamna

The questions that Rashi had asked me had stirred up a depth of memory that I had hoped I could leave behind me. I was reminded once again, whether I liked it or not, that it was the life that I had to come to terms with. Just because I was out of that horrible place didn't mean that all of it was behind me now. Not by a long shot.

Kabir sat there in silence with me for a long moment after Rashi left, and I found myself glad that he was nearby. It felt as though, whether we said a word or not, he was lifting some of the weight from my shoulders, taking a little of the burden from my mind.

"Would you like something to eat?" he asked awkwardly. "I know we just had breakfast, but I could make you something, if you like."

I pressed my fist to my stomach and found it grumbling. Back in that place, when I had been working for those men, they had only fed me when they'd remembered or when they'd felt like it. I could remember, vividly, lying in bed and staring at the ceiling with my stomach screaming at me, empty in a deep, profound way I hoped never to feel again. I felt like I had a hundred meals to make up for.

"I would love that." I smiled at him. "Can I help you?"

"I'm not sure it needs two sets of hands, but you can join me if you like," he replied, getting to his feet and offering me his hand. I hesitated for a moment, remembering the shock of discomfort that even Rashi's touch had sent through my body, but I took a deep breath and slipped my hand into his. It seemed to fit as though it had been made to go there, the two of us slotting together like pieces of a puzzle that had been built to fit next to one another.

He pulled me to my feet, and for a split second I was so close to him that I could have moved just an inch and kissed him. I could smell his aftershave, strong and masculine, like him. For a moment, it seemed to fill my senses to the very brim, overwhelming me. All thoughts slipped out of my mind, and I found my gaze drawn to his mouth – I could have leaned forward, just brushed my lips so gently against his. A thank-you kiss, I could tell myself. But I knew it was more than that. Being so close to him had suddenly stirred something in me, my stomach kindling with just the flicker of a flame. A flame that had been doused for so long that I had almost forgotten how it felt, but I recognised it there, as I stood an inch from him – desire… real, organic desire.

He stepped away from me before I could do anything, which was for the best. Anything happening between us would have been a mistake. I was such a mess, and I didn't want to inflict that on anybody else. And besides, I had only just taken my body back as my own. I didn't want to share it with anyone else until I knew I was ready.

He headed over to the kitchen, and I followed him. He got the makings of a salad out of the fridge and began chopping vegetables and measuring dressing. He would occasionally ask me to pass him something, and I did as I was told, pleased to feel like I was actually helping.

"I don't think I've ever really known a man who could cook before," I remarked, and he chuckled.

"It's not really cooking," he pointed out. "And I do have a cook who prepares most of my food for me."

"Yeah, I assumed you would need some staff to help run this place," I observed, glancing around.

"My parents would have this place full of staff if I let them," he shook his head fondly. "I keep telling them, I don't need so many people to look after me. I suppose they still think of me as their little boy."

"Well, you're certainly not that," I blurted before I could think about how flirtatious it would sound. He shot me a look, a smile, and I felt as though my heart was filling up in my chest, soaking up his attention.

"Can you pass me the coconut oil?" he pointed to a small container behind me, and I turned to grab it. When I passed it to him, our fingers touched for the briefest moment, and it was as though a small shock had passed from his fingertips to mine. I drew my hand away swiftly, trying to ignore the spark that felt as though it had prickled across every inch of my body at once.

He turned back to the salad and finished tossing it with the dressing. I watched the way his hands moved, the confidence with which he conducted himself in the kitchen. I felt my stomach grumbling once more, but there was another hunger inside me, something else that seemed to be brewing up and over deep within me. I did my best to ignore it for the time being as it was only going to complicate things. Besides, I had no idea how long I was actually going to be here; if a place in the shelter opened up, surely I would need to leave at once. I didn't want to be a burden on him, not more than I already had been. Sure, he was being nice to me now, but it would only be a matter of time until that changed and he decided he wanted to get rid of me. Just like all the men in my life had, at one point or another. Their kindness and patience ran out, no matter how sweet they may have seemed at the start.

He handed me a bowl, and I was so lost in thought that it took me a moment to realize what he was doing. I stared at it for a moment, and he raised his eyebrows at me, clearly a little amused by my blankness.

"You alright?" he asked, and I nodded quickly and took the bowl full of salad from him.

He led me back over to the sofa, and we sat there for a moment in silence before he reached to switch on the TV.

"I like to have it on in the background while I eat," he explained. "I'm not used to having company around here, you see."

"Oh?" I glanced around the place, surprised. I didn't remember much about my past from before they took me – my brain had blurred many of those memories out to dust in my mind, as though it knew it would be easier to cope with what was being inflicted on me if I had less to compare it to. But if I did remember some things correctly, a man with a home like this, who looked like that, and who could cook to boot should have had women beating down his door to get to him. I wondered why he was still single. Maybe he just hadn't found the right woman yet. Or maybe there was some darkness in him, the same darkness I had found hidden at the centre of so many of men I had served during my time in that place.

I heard a familiar burst of music from the television, and I swivelled around at once to face the screen. Upon it, a small family was crowded around a table, and I recognised the scene at once.

"Oh, this is *Masoom*!" I exclaimed in delight. "I loved this movie when I was a kid."

He grinned at me, clearly taken aback by the sudden display of emotion I had just come out with. I clapped my hand over my mouth. I had been taught that I should be seen and not heard for so long that I had forgotten what it was like not to be instantly scolded for expressing any kind of emotion at all.

"Sorry, I just haven't seen it in so long," I continued, lowering my voice a little. He shook his head.

"No, really, it's fine," he waved his hand and began serving us from the salad he had made. "You want to watch it? I've never seen it before."

"Oh, I'd love to," I gushed. "It's so good. And we've only missed the first five minutes..."

I sat back on the couch and began to gobble down the delicious food he had made for me. I didn't even know I was so hungry still. I felt warmth, sitting there with him, a warmth that felt so good it must have been false. I hadn't felt this way in such a long time that I found myself waiting for the carpet to be whipped from underneath me, for the curtains to fall away and reality to set in once more. But the film absorbed me quickly, bringing back distant memories of crowding around the television with my family to sing along to the songs and practically chant along with the scenes we'd seen a thousand times. Something ached in me, deep down, for the family that felt like blurred-out shadows in my memory. But for the time being, I just allowed myself to be absorbed by the movie playing.

I snuck looks at Kabir at a few points, and I found him smiling along to what was playing out in front of him. I noticed him shift a couple of times, to move an inch or two closer to me, and I once again caught the scent of his aftershave and found myself drawn back to the memory of his body so close to mine, when I had been so tempted to kiss him that it had taken everything in me not to just go ahead and do it. Even now, sitting here opposite him, I just wanted to – I didn't know what I wanted to do, but I had a feeling that the women he'd grown up around, the ones he'd known most of his life, certainly didn't do it, so I held back. How did women act, out here in the real world? I had so much to learn, being an adult here for the first time in my life. I hoped he would be able to guide me through it. There was something so comfortingly normal about Kabir. I knew that if I was going to learn how to do this properly, it was going to be from him.

To my surprise, I found myself getting drowsy again, not long after I'd eaten. The kind of warm, safe, comfortable sleepiness that descends after a good meal, and only when you're in the company that allows you to feel that secure. As the familiar scenes played out in front of me, I let my eyes drift shut, an enormous yawn escaping from my mouth before I could stop it. I went to apologize for my rudeness, but before I could, sleep took me and I sank into a peaceful rest.

I wasn't sure how long I was asleep for; when I opened my eyes once more, the film had finished, and Kabir was watching something else. I woke because of a touch – it took me a moment to figure out where it was coming from and what it was doing to me deep in my belly. I felt an automatic panic response. Something in me was screaming at me to leap up and get out, and it took me a moment to remember my current position, to convince myself that I was safe and that nobody here planned to hurt me.

Then the touch came again, and I finally figured out what the source was. As my eyes fluttered all the way open and I rose back into reality once more, I realized that I was lying down on the couch. I had shifted around in my sleep, and now my head was resting in Kabir's lap, on his knees, on top of a pillow that he must have laid there for me. My heart ached at his sweetness as I took in what he had done; instead of pushing me off or carting me away to my bed, he had let me rest here for a while as the intensity of the last few days began to wear off. His gentle fingers, working their way over my scalp, brushing through my hair in a regular, gentle pattern. I closed my eyes again and allowed myself to get lost to the sensation of it. I was surprised at how good it felt, given that even Rashi's touch earlier had been enough to send my panic systems launching into high gear. But his gentleness, his tenderness – even his absent-mindedness, as though it hadn't even crossed his mind not to do this – they were calming me, soothing me in a way that I hadn't known I needed.

I let myself lay there for a long while, not bothering to concentrate on what was on the TV in front of me. I couldn't have cared less. It had been so long since anyone had really touched me with the goal of anything other than the satisfaction of their selfish desires, that even this, this mild tenderness, was enough to send my head spinning to infinity.

I wasn't sure how long it was before I moved, before he noticed that my eyes were open. And everything changed in an instant.

He didn't leap to his feet, not quite – he wasn't that rough with me. In fact, he lifted the pillow carefully off his lap first, sending me jerking upright in surprise at the suddenness of his movement. When I looked into his eyes, I saw something etched there that I couldn't make sense of. Guilt, perhaps? It seemed to run deeper than that. He would hardly look at me, keeping his eyes trained on the TV as he went to turn it off.

"I'm sorry, I didn't mean to…" He bumped into the table, sending the plates juddering against the wood. I would have giggled if it wasn't for the dead-serious look on his face.

"It's okay, really." I tried to soothe him, but he was clearly perturbed, his still waters suddenly stormy.

"No, I should get…" He gathered all the plates swiftly and headed to the kitchen. I could still feel the paths his fingers had followed in my hair, and I reached up to trace them myself, but it just wasn't the same. I wanted him to come back, to hold me as he just had, but he seemed unsettled, as though he thought that he shouldn't have been touching me like that.

My heart fell as the realization sank in. Is that how he saw me? As some delicate creature that he had to tiptoe around. He viewed me as damaged goods. And perhaps that was the truth of it. Perhaps he was right to hold me at arm's length.

I got to my feet, wrapping my arms around myself protectively. He snuck a look at me as he put away the dishes. He must have had a cleaner – he said there was some staff around– so the only reason for him to be doing that would be to avoid me for a moment longer.

"I'm going to bed," I excused myself. I didn't want to impose on him any longer. I thought back to waking up on his lap, and wondered how he could have let himself get there if he was clearly so unsettled by it. It didn't make sense to me.

"I'll see you later," he murmured and nodded, voice gruff. I lingered for a moment longer, hoping he would speak again and ask me to stay, but he didn't. So I turned and made my way into my room, closing the door tight behind. I fell forward onto my bed, a near-comical childish frown on my face. Why had he pulled away from me so quickly? And why, exactly, had I wanted him to hold me like that all day and all night long? The questions spun around my head, and I knew sleep would be hard to find that night.

5

Kabir

As I watched Aamna reading on the couch, I wondered how much more wrong I could have been about her.

When Rashi had told me that she was bringing a woman who had worked as an escort, to my home, I had imagined… well, I had pictured all those classic images of women who sold their bodies for money – overdressed, talons for nails, make-up that looked a couple of inches deep. And a hard-edged personality, one that they had cultivated in order to keep themselves safe and removed from their work. But Aamna didn't fit into any of that, and I was beginning to wonder just how many other notions I'd had about her would turn out to be wrong, too.

I had been spending a lot of time with her lately, especially after Rashi had begged me to take some time away from work to look after her.

"I'm not saying it's going to be for long," she had said over the phone, and I could hear the blare of traffic down her end of the line. I was in the office, just returned from a meeting with a potential new director we wanted to get on board, and even the thought of being caught in the rush hour made me wince.

"But you need me to do it anyway," I finished up for her with a long sigh.

"It's just that all the girls down at the shelter have people with them twenty-four-seven," she explained. "And I don't want Aamna to miss out on that. These first few weeks, they're the most important when it comes to getting her back into society, and if we mess that up..."

She trailed off, and she didn't need to finish up what she was saying. I understood. I looked around my office – even though I had been working in this office for almost three months now, I had never bothered decorating the place with trinkets or posters or pictures. It was still just as blank and bland as the first day I had moved in. Maybe spending some time with a real human being, instead of sitting around in this carefully-cultivated dead space, would do me some good.

"I get it," I agreed, and I began to pace up and down the office. "But how long do you think it's going to be for? How long should I tell them I'll be gone for?"

"Just tell them you're taking some time off," I could practically see the furrow in her brow as she spoke. "You're the boss, Kabir. You can do whatever you want."

"Our parents will find out about it," I warned her, and she fell silent for a moment. It was clear that the thought of our parents hadn't necessarily crossed her mind.

"Yeah, well, let them," she replied firmly. "I'll deal with them when and if they turn up. I just need you to do this for now, alright?"

"I will, Rashi," I promised her. "As soon as I get finished up today, I'll organize some people to cover for me while I'm away and I'll take care of her."

"Thank you," Rashi let out a long breath, the static rushing down the line. "I really appreciate this. And I know it might not seem like she does at the moment, but I promise she will, Kabir. She's still coming back down to earth, after all."

"Right," I agreed, not knowing what else to say to that.

Aamna had been living with me for almost two weeks, and I had to admit, while I would rather have been at the family business handling everything that came in, it was good to take a breather and step back from that place for a while. Even if it was only a matter of time before one of my parents caught on to the fact that I wasn't at work and came storming down here to figure out what the hell was going on. They let Rashi do what she wanted, let her engage with these projects of hers, but I had a feeling that if they found out I was involved, they would be less than impressed. I knew they saw Rashi's work as less and mine as legitimate, and knowing that she had coaxed me into joining her on her *(un)*worthy moral crusade might annoy them. Honestly, if I was being truthful with myself, I was glad to have a chance to spend more time with this woman, because she utterly fascinated me.

She seemed to be built entirely from contradiction. She had seen so much, been through so much, but she never spoke a word of it to me or anyone else. She had been forced to sell her body for sex, and yet every chance she got, she covered up and hid herself. She had spent years locked away with no real education or stimulation, and yet every chance she got, she would have a book in her hand or be watching a movie or flicking through a newspaper. It was like she was trying to find a way back into the world that she had been hidden from for so long, and I had to be the one to guide her out into the light.

I was making myself tea as I watched her on the couch that morning, her legs kicked out over the arm as she lay sideways on the cushions. Her eyes were scanning across the pages hurriedly, as though she couldn't get the words into her head fast enough. I couldn't help but smile. Her hair was pulled back into a ponytail at the back of her head, as though anything that would get in the way of her reading would be a negative.

"Do you want a cup of tea?" I offered, and she glanced up at me and blinked, as though she had forgotten that I was there. After a moment, she nodded and smiled.

"I would love one," she agreed, and she propped herself up, leaning on the back of the couch as she watched me. She did this a lot, watch and observe me – as though she was making sure I wasn't about to do something unexpected. I made sure to move slowly, giving her plenty of time to get used to the way I moved my hands, my body. I noticed that she was staring at my fingers, and something about her gaze was ambiguous to me and made the tips of my fingers tingle.

"What are you going to do today?" I asked her, distracting myself from the thoughts running through my head. She shrugged and shook her head.

"I don't know," she replied, and then she opened her mouth and closed it again, like she had something to say but was a little embarrassed to say it.

"What is it?" I prompted her.

"There's a movie on tonight that I want to see," she told me, "On the television. But… it's a horror movie, and I don't want to watch it by myself…"

She looked at me expectantly, and it took me a moment to realize that she was asking me to watch it with her. The thought of the two of us on the couch together – maybe her holding my hand, burying her face in my shoulder to hide from the scares…

"I'll watch it with you," I nodded, trying to keep my face neutral. "What time is it on?"

"Seven," she glanced at the clock above the television and smiled. I came around the counter and handed her a mug of tea.

"Thank you." She smiled at me, and our fingertips brushed for the briefest moment as she took the cup from me. I did my best to ignore the shiver of sensation that ran down my spine as our skin connected, and turned to head back to my home office.

"I'll see you at seven," I announced and glanced over my shoulder to see her grinning and picking up her book once more. It might have been a big chunk of my evening to give up, but if I was being honest, I would have given up a whole week if it meant getting to see that look written all over her face.

I joined her that evening for the movie and found that she had brought the blanket from her room and wrapped it around herself. She looked nervous but excited; she was chattier than usual, as though trying to distract herself from the scares she knew were coming.

"I used to love horror movies," she recounted. "But I never got to watch them, because I was so young and I get scared so easily. My mother—"

She stopped herself dead before she went any further, and her mouth turned downward into a frown suddenly. I reached out to touch her knee, drawing her back to the real world.

"Aamna?" I murmured her name. "Are you alright?"

"Yes, I just..." She trailed off and furrowed her brow. "I just... I just can't remember."

She fell silent for a moment, and I realized my hand was still on her knee and withdrew it swiftly. The last thing I needed was a repeat of the first week when she had snuggled into my lap, and I had just let her sleep there. I got up to switch off the lights as the movie began and, lit by the glow of the television, I tried my hardest not to notice how beautiful she looked.

She enjoyed the movie, and managed to stay awake through the whole thing – there were a couple of jump-scares that had her grasping for my arm or my hand, but I made sure that every time she touched me, she was the one initiating it. Even though I just wanted to pull her into my arms, hold her close, inhale that sweet scent that seemed to come off her in waves, I couldn't. I wouldn't! She barely knew me, and after everything she had already been through, the last thing she needed was another man who desired her in that way.

She enjoyed watching the movie with me so much that she asked me, shyly, if I would join her for another one the next day. And I agreed. Because it was time I got to spend alone with her, and I had found myself craving that in a way I had never imagined I would. She was quiet, but then, so was I, and sharing these couple of hours a night where we could focus on a constructed reality, talk about the acting and directing and cinematography, it was a chance for us to connect without having to do it in the rawness of the real world. I knew she felt safe in fiction, in a way she never had in the last few years of her exploitation, and I was happy to guide her into it, let her lose herself in the warmth and comfort of the unreal. Maybe I needed it more than I would have cared to admit.

And those evenings started off quiet, with both of us chuckling at the jokes or occasionally offering a comment on some particularly egregious performance. However, before I knew it, we would be having full-blown conversations. A place would turn up in the movie where one or both of us had travelled to, and we would share our memories of it. Some character in the movie would bite into a food that would make us both cringe, and suddenly we would be discussing the best things to eat and the things we couldn't even stand to look at. And when the movie was finished, we would exchange opinions, recommendations, what we thought we should watch next. Then she would go to her bed, and I would go to mine, and I would lay awake and wonder how wrong it would be to slip through there and join her.

But I kept these thoughts out of my mind as best as I could, because I knew that Rashi would eat me alive if she found out that I had developed a crush on Aamna. And really, how much of a crush was it? Sure, she was beautiful and sweet, and she had this dry sense of humour that sometimes made me burst out laughing when I least expected it, but surely my feelings for her grew more from the fact that I wanted to protect her than anything else. Or maybe I really had feelings for her and was desperately trying to intellectualize my way out of it.

One night, after we had watched a bad romantic comedy that we had laughed all the way through, we were both in our respective beds, I heard a noise. It sounded like a squeak. I sat up straight in bed, looking around, trying to figure out where it was coming from. The stillness seemed to hold its breath around me, and I sank back down into the sheets, assuming it was some trick of my mind or some noise from the street outside.

And then it came again, longer this time, and shifting into a groan as it went. And then it struck me – it was coming from Aamna's room.

My heart punched up in my chest, and my pulse kicked into a high gear as I rolled out of my bed and strode through to her room. My mind was flooded with the images of the men who had exploited her, somehow finding her and taking her back, taking her away from me.

I pushed the door open and found the room empty, except for her – she was lying flat on her bed, and her face was twisted into a mask of fear and anger. She let out another noise again, this awful sound, as though there was a monster inside her, trying to claw its way up and out of her body.

"Aamna," I murmured. "Aamna, wake up!"

She made another noise and flopped her body away from me; she was trembling and twitching, like she was attempting to fight off some attacker in her head. I went over to her, laid a hand on her shoulder.

"Aamna," I tried once more, but it didn't work. She was shaking so much that the entire bed was rocking around her, and the noises were growing, growling groans of what sounded like terror rising from within her.

"Aamna," I squeezed her arm. "It's me; it's Kabir, wake—"

And with that, her eyes flew open and her gaze fell on me, and she froze on the bed for a moment. For that instant, I was sure that I had overstepped my bounds, that I had invaded her space – but then she moved towards me, throwing herself into my arms, clutching on to my shoulders like I was the only thing keeping her pinned to earth.

I sank on to the bed and just held her for a long while. I would have done it all night if she had needed me to, but as it was, I sat there for a few minutes, slowly rocking her back and forth, listening to her breath as it turned from tearing gasps into something slower, steadier. Her nails were digging into my shoulders, and it was only then that I realized I was naked from the waist up, sleeping in only a pair of sweatpants. She was just wearing a shirt, her bare legs drawn up to her chest, and I tried my best to ignore how nice her skin felt against mine.

"Are you alright?" I murmured softly, holding her close. She nodded, slowly, but didn't pull away from me.

"Just a bad dream," she managed. Her voice was so tiny that it took me a moment to realize she was talking at all.

"You're safe here," I told her firmly, and I was surprised by the fervour in my voice; I really wanted her to believe that, to prove it to her any way I could if I had to. She pulled back and looked at me, her eyes still a little distant, as though she was coming down from another plane.

"I know," she murmured, and she leaned into me once more, pressing her head into my chest, as though she was listening to the beat of my heart.

I wasn't sure how long we stayed like that, but eventually, I felt her breathing smooth out and deepen as she fell asleep in my arms once more, just like she had done on the couch that time. There was something almost painfully intimate about the fact that she trusted me enough to let me hold her like this, even at her most vulnerable. I had no idea what the nightmare had been about, but it had been enough to shake her – and I had been enough to soothe her, it seemed.

I gently lay her down on the bed and tucked her in beneath the covers, and brushed her hair back from her face. I was suddenly drawn to plant a kiss on her forehead, but that would have been a step too far. With one last lingering look at her, I carefully stepped out of the bedroom and pulled the door shut behind me, and climbed back into my own bed. The scent of her was all over me, and as I closed my eyes and let sleep take me once more, I could fool myself into thinking she was there, lying beside me.

I woke early the next morning, and heard her already moving around in the kitchen. I pulled on some clothes and climbed out of bed, heading through to check if she was alright.

"Hi," she smiled at me, a little nervously as she made herself a cup of tea. "Would you like one?"

"Love one," I replied, and I leaned on the counter and watched her as she moved with some confidence around the kitchen. I couldn't remember her ever coming in here when I wasn't around, and this had to be a step forward. She was beginning to learn how to take care of herself once more, and that could only be a good thing.

She handed me my mug – she had noticed the one I liked best and made sure to use it – and took a seat at the breakfast bar, tucking her legs up and underneath her, and watching me for a moment.

"What is it?" I asked. I could still almost feel her in my arms – how delicate she had felt, how easily breakable. It had stirred something in me, something intense, and I was doing my best to tamp it down now. But the way she was looking at me wasn't helping.

She took a deep breath, as though she had been figuring out how to say this for a long time, and then spoke.

"It's been…" she began, halted, shook her head at herself, and then started again. "It's been such a long time since anyone held me like that."

The words were stark and simple, but they instantly seared themselves into my brain, as though she had burned them there. I wasn't sure what I was meant to say to that. I wanted to tell her that I would have held her all night long if that's what she wanted, that I would have lain there with her all night and held her in my arms until she felt safe enough to fall asleep, until the bad dream had retreated once more. But I couldn't find the words.

She stepped off the chair and moved around the side of the counter. Before I could move away from her, an instinct I had cultivated in myself to keep myself from getting too close to her, she leaned and planted a kiss on my cheek.

"Thank you," she murmured, hovering near me for a moment longer, and then she turned and walked out of the room and left me staring at my tea and trying to make sense of the mess of feeling that her kiss had raised in me.

I returned to my office and shut the door behind me, sitting down in front of my computer. I stared at the screen for a moment, knowing that I had plenty of emails to reply to and plenty of work to catch up on. But all I could focus on was the feel of her lips against my skin. I touched my finger to my cheek, as though mimicking the sensation of her mouth there just moments before. And I knew, right there and then, that this crush ran deeper than I ever would have liked to admit to myself.

I tried to remember the last time I had felt this way. The last person I had seriously dated had been Chhaya and that – well, the less we said about that, the better it was. Things with Chhaya had never been perfect and had swiftly taken a sharp downturn into downright terrible. My experience with her had been enough to put me off dating entirely ever since. But then, that was mainly because I never found a woman who didn't resemble Chhaya in some way. Every woman I met or tried to consider reminded me of her in some way. But Aamna didn't. She had a certain softness to her, her hard edges imperceptible. There was a compassion that came off her in waves.

That evening, we had planned to watch the sequel to a movie we had enjoyed together a few days before, and though I did not want to be closer to her anymore, I was helpless. I knew that if I were to try and find a way to get out of it, she would figure it out instantly. So I hid out in my room and worked all day, hoping that I would be able to scrub the memory of her kiss out of my mind with enough banality, until she knocked on the door and called to me.

"Kabir?"

The sound of her speaking my name ignited something inside of me; something deep in my belly, something I hadn't felt for anyone in a long time. I did my best to dampen it and then got to my feet to greet her.

"Hi," she smiled as I opened the door. "The movie's about to start. Do you still want to watch it with me?"

As I looked down at her, I knew that I should have told her that I had too much work, that I was too busy that day, that I needed a little time to myself. I should have taken time away from her to cool off, to stop the whip of feeling for her growing any more intense. But I didn't want to. I craved her company, her presence, the sound of her voice – her touch, her kiss.

"Sure," I nodded, and I followed her to the couch. It seemed smaller than before as she curled up at one end, and I felt like wherever I sat, I was going to be dangerously close to her.

The movie started, and I stole a glance at her and found her watching the screen intently. Of course, she was. She probably hadn't spent the whole day in torment, trying to figure out how she felt about me. Aamna was probably only focused on being safe, being here and being far from what she had known all this time. Her kiss was an expression of thanks, not desire. My gaze was drawn to the delicate anklet around her perfect leg, the way the glimmering metal hung from her was mesmerizing. And all I wanted to do was touch it, to trace the shape of it with my fingers. To trace the shape of her, to learn her contours, her dips and shadows, and shapes.

I turned my attention back to the movie, but I was hyper-aware of Aamna and every move she made. She shifted closer to me a couple of times, eyes still trained on the screen in front of her, and I wanted nothing more than to draw her in close to me. I fought the urge. It was harder than I had ever imagined it would be. I could still remember, vividly, how good she had felt in my arms, how natural it had seemed for me to hold her that way.

Our bodies were so close that I could have shifted an inch and been touching her. Is that what she wanted? A strand of her hair slipped down over her face, and without thinking, I brushed it back for her, as I had done the night before when she had fallen asleep.

Before I could draw my hand away, she caught it between her own, and I felt as though my heart was going to stop dead in my chest. The sounds of the movie dulled to nothing in my ears, and I just looked at her, looked into the eyes of the woman that I knew now, more than ever, that I was falling for.

She moved closer to me and now her legs were resting in my lap. The weight of her small, soft body against mine stirred me. I couldn't hide from it anymore. What had begun with her pressing her lips to my cheek that morning was coming to life, and I wanted to lean into it.

"Aamna..." I began, not sure what I was going to say but knowing I needed to say something. I desired her, wanted her in a way that I couldn't remember wanting anyone before in my entire life, but she was so hurt, so damaged. I didn't want her to think that she had to do this, or that she owed it to me. She leaned forward and brushed her finger over my lips, hushing me.

"Kabir, I want this," she murmured, her eyes bright and sincere even in the dark. "I want... I want you."

And as soon as those words came out of her mouth, any resistance I might have been holding on to fell away at once, and I leaned forward and kissed her for the first time.

Her mouth was so soft and so sweet that for a moment, everything else dropped away and that sensation was the only thing I could focus on. She let out the softest moan as our lips met, and I grasped her head between my hands and held her close, as though trying to affirm to myself that this was truly happening.

I guided her on top of me, reaching over to flick the TV off. As I did, so she gripped the top of my shirt in her fingers as she lay down upon me. I couldn't get over how small she felt, how delicate – how a creature like her could have so much impact on me, could swell to take up all this space inside my head. I ran my hands through her hair, down her neck, tracing my fingers over the shape of her shoulders and her spine. She wriggled against me, letting out another little moan of pleasure, and I felt myself stirring to hardness. I had waited so long to touch her like this, and now it was finally happening, my body seemed to want to move into fast-forward.

But I was determined to make the most of this. I wanted to learn every inch of her, to commit her to memory; as we kissed, she ran her fingers over my neck, my chin, my scalp, as though she had the same thoughts running through her head. I moved my hands down, over her waist, feeling the curve as it extended out into her hips and her thighs. As our legs tangled, I could feel her anklet pressing against my skin. It had been one of the first things I had ever noticed about her; the first time I had noticed her beauty.

I held her like I had the night before, but this time she was giving back to me, her body receptive to mine. I slipped my tongue into her mouth, and she balled her hands in my hair, tugging slightly, moving her body with more purpose against my own. I sank my fingers into her hips and pulled her against me so I could feel every inch of her on top of me.

She moved down and brushed her mouth over my neck, and I groaned and tipped my head back, craving more. She giggled softly as she kissed up my throat, to that spot right where my ear met my neck, the one that made the fire in my belly burn brighter than ever before.

Her lips found my mouth once more, and I moved and rolled so that I was on top of her. She parted her legs at once and hooked them around my back, pulling me on to her with more passion. Her breath was coming fast, her chest rising and falling swiftly as I pulled the shirt up and over her head, tossing it aside. She was naked beneath it, and I sat back for a moment to admire her.

"You're so beautiful," I murmured, and she closed her eyes and let out a long breath. Her eyes were dark with desire, her lips slightly parted as though she craved my kiss once more, and I brushed my fingers across her mouth as she had done to me earlier. She flicked her tongue out to meet me, tracing the shape of my thumb for a moment.

I moved down to kiss her again, unable to resist, but this time began to work down her body, over her chin, baring my teeth against her throat, and then further, further, until I could take her nipple between my lips, tease her with my tongue. She gasped, and I stole a glance at her and found her eyes closed, and her head tipped back as though she had utterly given over to the pleasure I was giving her.

She ran her fingers through my hair and held me in place as I moved to her other breast to tantalize her with my tongue. I noticed that her chest was rising and falling with more insistence than before, as though the desire was trying to burst up and out of her. Moving my hand down, I skimmed it over her belly, that soft, sensitive part right below her navel, and then slipped it down and into her soft cotton underwear.

"Kabir..." she groaned, and for a second I thought she was going to ask me to stop, that this was too much, too soon, and that she needed me to hold back. But when I looked up at her again, it was as though she had been speaking me into existence with her words, reminding herself who she was with right now, who was touching her. I let my fingers slip down, finding her wetness, and she let out a long moan as I traced against her sensitive nub. I went slow, gentle, letting her set the pace, and she began to slowly rock her hips back and forth so that she could grind against my hand. I found myself growing needy, the pressure between my legs getting more intense as she used me like this – her head was tipping back and forth, her eyes closed and her mouth opening and closing like she was trying to give shape to some wordless pleasure deep inside of her.

I shifted my body back up on top of her so I could kiss her once more, and she swiftly wound her arms around my neck and pulled me close, her embrace more ferocious than it had been the last time. I dipped my fingers down, tracing her entrance, and she gasped against my mouth. I pulled back to check if she was alright, and her eyes burned into mine with a need I had never seen before.

"I want…" she breathed, and she continued to move her hips against me, attempting to convey without words what it was she wanted me to do. But I needed to hear it from her. All of this had to happen on her terms, no matter how badly I wanted her.

"I want you inside of me," she finally murmured, and the words sent an intense desire spiralling through my body. I was glad she wanted me now because I wasn't sure how much longer I could have taken touching her like this. I wanted to take my time, to learn each and every curve and contour of her body, but that could come after we had shared ourselves with each other in the most intimate way.

I got to my feet and lifted her into my arms, cradling her close to my chest, and she planted a line of kisses up my neck as I carried her to the bedroom. I lay her down gently on the covers, and she quickly kicked off her jeans and her underwear so that she was lying there, bare naked, waiting for me. Her eyes burned into me, and I could barely look at her, I was so overwhelmed with lust. I wasn't sure I would be able to control myself if I took a look at her like that, splayed on the bed, waiting for me, hungry for me.

I quickly stripped down myself, and grabbed a condom from the bedside table to sheathe myself; she skimmed her fingers over my back as she waited for me, and it was like she was leaving a little trail of fire wherever she touched me. Like she was branding me, burning herself into me.

I glided on top of her, and she hooked her arms around my neck and pulled me eagerly; lips slightly parted, she kissed me again, our tongues meeting with an urgent hunger that consumed everything else. She pressed her hips up against me, and I guided my erection against her. She inhaled deeply as I moved slowly into her for the first time. I wrapped her tight in my arms and pushed into her as far as I could go.

The feeling then was far more than physical, though those sensations were incredible enough; her warmth, her tightness, her slickness, and the way she arched her back to take me deeper. The feeling of her connecting with me like this, knowing that she wanted me as deeply as I wanted her, was what took control of me. I had spent so much time with this woman, this woman who had come to me in pieces, and it felt as though both of us were putting ourselves back together with this – or maybe building something else, something entirely new.

She crossed her ankles behind my back and drew me into her, and I needed no encouragement. I inhaled her scent as I buried my face into her neck, holding her close as she began to tremble with pleasure, as her muscles began to tense. I wasn't sure how long we held each other like that, time seeming to drop away as I thrust into her, but soon I felt myself filling with pleasure, my body craving that release once and for all.

She fisted her hand in my hair and tugged me back, so that I was looking at her, just in time to see her face contort as she found her release – a shiver ran across her entire body, her mouth opening, her eyes blazing, and the sight of her lost to such pleasure pushed me over the edge. She didn't take her eyes off mine as it happened, as we both climaxed mere seconds apart, and the image of her face like that seared itself into my brain as though I ever would have forgotten her otherwise.

A moment later, I slipped out of her and went to dispose of the condom. When I came back to the bedroom, I found her curled on her side, still on top of the covers, angled towards the door so I couldn't see her face.

"Are you alright?" I asked, tentatively, as I lay down on my bed next to her. I laid my hand gently on her hip, and instead of jumping or pulling away, she nodded. She finally turned to look at me and smiled.

"Yes," she promised me, her tone certain, and I moved into her, curling my body around hers. And I felt a sudden, overwhelming sense of protectiveness. In that moment, I would have fought for her in any way I had to. To earn this moment, her in my arms, safe and content, there wasn't anything in the world I wouldn't have done for her. I closed my eyes and nestled my face into her hair, and prayed that nothing would happen to force me to find out how far I would go for her.

6

Aamna

I woke up, and for a moment a start of terror ran through me. I didn't recognize the room that I was in. I had never woken up here before. I wasn't in that bedroom that Kabir had given me; I was somewhere else – back at the brothel? No, I couldn't be. This didn't look right. I couldn't—

Before the panic could take control of me, I heard a noise from the other side of the bed, and I turned to find Kabir snuffling slightly in his sleep. I smiled and closed my eyes, and let my head sink back into the pillow. Yes, I remembered now, the night before, the two of us, we had... we had done that; for the first time. And it had been incredible.

I lay there in bed, next to him, not wanting to get up and disturb him. I reached over to brush a strand of hair back from his face, and he shifted closer to me, slipping his arm over my waist to pull me closer. I could still remember when a touch like that would have sent me into a tailspin of panic and fear, but I didn't feel any of that when I was with him.

I wasn't sure I would ever be able to do what we had done last night with anyone ever again. At least, I wasn't sure that I would be able to enjoy it. For so long, my sexuality and my body had belonged to whoever had paid for me, whoever wanted to use me for as long as they wanted to, and I had grown so disconnected from my desires, from what I truly wanted. But Kabir was gentle, let me set the pace, listened to me and asked me and checked in on me. He was a caring lover, sweeter than any man I had been with before, and he wasn't doing this because he had paid for me and wanted to get his money's worth – he was doing this because he wanted me, organically, properly, truly. And I wanted him the same way. I felt a flood of panic run through me, unbidden. And I knew that it was ridiculous because I couldn't remember being happier with anyone before in my life. But now that I had this, it could be ripped away from me. I could almost feel Shekhar's face in my mind, his touch, and that grasping ownership he insisted on taking from me. No matter how many times I had tried to blot it out, it had still made an impression on me, pressing down on my mind like a branding. The way Shekhar used to look at me, I had been sure that he saw me as his lover, as his equal. I could never figure out how he could believe that, given what he was doing to me, and it was that faux-romance that scared me the most. Now I knew what the real thing was, the thought of returning back there terrified me.

Kabir stirred awake beside me, and leaned over to plant a kiss on my arm. I smiled and pushed away all the vile thoughts that had shoved back in my mind. I wasn't there anymore. That was all that mattered. It was in the past now.

"Good morning, you," he murmured, a little blearily. He looked so cute when he had just woken up, his face a little crumpled from the pillow and his hair messy. When I'd met him, when I'd first come to this place, I would never have imagined that someone who seemed so buttoned-up could be so casual and sweet.

"Good morning to you too." I smiled, and I slipped down in bed so I could look him right in the eye. I wanted to remember this moment. I never wanted it to end. If I could have set up shop and just lived here for the rest of my life, I would have done just that.

"I'm hungry," he remarked. "You want something to eat?"

"I would love that," I agreed, and he yawned and climbed out of bed. I smiled as I watched him gather his clothes, enjoying his nakedness even more in the light of day.

"Let me fetch your clothes through for you, and I'll get the cook to make something for us," he told me. "Don't worry about getting out of bed yet."

"I won't," I agreed, and, as though he couldn't resist it, he moved towards me and planted a kiss on my temple. I grinned.

"Be back in a minute," he murmured and wandered out to go get us something to eat. I lay back against the luxurious pillows and turned my attention to the window, which looked down on to the city beyond. There was so much out there for me, so much that I had never seen, so much that had been kept from me as I had been trapped up in that awful place.

Like my family. My family was still out there somewhere. The corners of my mouth turned down, and I furrowed my brow as I considered them. What did they think had happened to me? Had they gone looking for me, or had they assumed I'd left under my own steam? Did they still live in the city, or had my vanishing driven them out of the house I'd grown up in?

"Aamna?"

I glanced up, and I found Kabir waiting in the doorway with a large tray that was laden with breakfast food, anything I could have wanted – fruit, pastries, juice, coffee, tea. How long had I been gazing out of that window? Sometimes it felt like when I retreated inside my own head, time could pass so quickly that I couldn't keep up with it. I blinked and brought myself back to reality. I could figure out what I was going to do about my family later. For now, I just wanted to enjoy this, the intimacy of waking up with Kabir, his sweetness after what we had done the night before.

"I wasn't sure what you want, so I got a little of everything." He shrugged, perching on the edge of the bed and laying the tray down carefully. "Eat as much as you want. I know I worked up an appetite last night."

"Thank you." I flashed him a smile and started into the food, pouring myself a glass of juice and sipping on it.

"What would you like to do today?" he asked, cocking his head at me. I shrugged and shook my head.

"I really don't know," I admitted. "I've never… I mean, I've never had a day free like this. I don't really know what is out there for me to do."

"Anything you want." He shrugged. "We could go to a movie, go out for dinner, and take a drive around the city…"

He must have seen the look on my face because he stopped himself and smiled at me.

"Or we could just spend the day here," he suggested, "Movies and… well, anything else that happens."

"That sounds perfect," I agreed at once. He grabbed a coffee and took up a spot on the bed next to me while I ate. He was quiet, but I was comfortable with it. After a few minutes, his phone rang.

"Excuse me," he got to his feet and went to take the call, and I watched him as he went. He was being so sweet to me. There was a part of me, a part that had been cultivated by what I had been through, that felt as though… as though I was unworthy of this kind of sweetness and I hadn't done enough to warrant this gentlemanly kindness. I knew that was ridiculous, but it would take a long time to unlearn the bullshit that had been poured into my ear when I had been trafficked. Even using that word felt foreign to me.

Kabir came back into the room, and he had a furrow in his brow.

"Everything okay?" I asked nervously, and he nodded.

"Yeah, Rashi just said she's got some news, and she's dropping by soon," he replied. "I think she wants to speak to you."

"And I guess I should probably be out of your bed by the time she gets here, right?" I teased him gently, and he grinned and nodded.

"I think it would be best if she didn't know exactly what had happened between us," he remarked. "At least, not yet. She's got enough on her mind already."

"Agreed," I nodded. I too wanted to keep what had happened the night before between just me and Kabir. That way, I could hold on to that intimacy, to how good it felt to be wrapped up in this little bubble of safety and tenderness. I finished up what I had been eating, and got to my feet. I was still naked, and for a moment felt a flicker of awkwardness at being so bare – but then I saw the way he was looking at me, and I giggled.

"Make it a little less obvious, would you?" I teased him again, and he held his hands up and averted his gaze.

"Sorry, but when you look like that…" he replied, and I went to get dressed in the clothes he had brought for me. If I'd had my way, I would have spent the whole day in his bed without putting on a single scrap of clothing, but it might have been a bit of a giveaway if Rashi had found me naked in his bed. Maybe just a little.

I washed up and headed through to the living room to wait for Kabir's sister, while Kabir took care of the bedroom and tidied up. I listened to the sound of his footfalls and smiled to myself. Rashi came to the door, and Kabir let her in at once. She gave him a hug and raked her hand through her hair and turned to me.

"I'll give you guys some space," Kabir backed out of the room and back into the bedroom, and he flashed me a secret, special smile that my heart almost burst from fullness. I returned it as Rashi hung up her coat, and then she came over to sit next to me on the couch.

"So, how are you doing, Aamna?" she asked with a gentle smile. She had to be one of the kindest women I'd ever met – her and her brother both, they reflected the same deep compassion, that ability to connect and care for people so far removed from them. I nodded.

"I'm actually feeling okay," I told her truthfully, and I glanced towards Kabir's door. I wished he could have been here with me, but we couldn't say for sure that Rashi wouldn't pick up on something between us if we were in the same room together.

"Well, I have some good news for you." She smiled. "There's room for you at the shelter now. We finally have the free space for you, so you can come down tomorrow and get settled in."

"Oh!" I furrowed my brow. My stomach twisted into a knot. "I didn't realize it would be so soon."

"You've already been here nearly a month," she reminded me. "I'm just sorry I had to stick you here for so long. Without the kind of support you really need."

I opened and closed my mouth. I couldn't believe this was happening, especially the night after we had made love for the first time. Just a few moments before, my future with Kabir had stretched out endlessly, no finality in sight, and now Rashi was sitting in front of me and telling me that it was all over.

"I know that it's a pain having to move down to a new place," she continued, noticing my hesitation. "But it's for the best. Kabir can get back to his work, and you can get the support you need."

I fell silent once more. Kabir had been taking a lot of time away from his real life for me. And I knew he would keep doing that as long as I was still around. He deserved his space again, away from me. I wasn't a reality for him; I was an escape from it. And I couldn't do that forever. Rashi was right – to get better, I needed real help. I couldn't put it all on Kabir; expect him to make me whole again, no matter how much I believed that he could.

"Right, okay," I nodded. "Tomorrow morning?"

"Evening," she corrected. "We'll send someone around to pick you up, and then you'll be at the shelter in time for dinner."

"Is it far from here?" I asked.

"About a half-hour drive," she replied. My stomach felt as though it was dropping down to my shoes. The thought of being that far away from him, after what we had just shared…

"Are you alright, Aamna?" Rashi asked. "You seem a little out of sorts."

"Just tired, that's all," I lied swiftly. "I didn't get a lot of sleep last night."

"Well, hopefully, you'll be able to rest a little easier in the shelter," she assured me. "We have security there, and counsellors on twenty-four-seven call, so if you ever need someone to talk to, or just to sit with you, we have people there."

I nodded again. This was all happening so fast that I could barely keep up with it. I wanted to tell her, no, I was staying here with Kabir, but that would only have been a further imposition on him after I had asked for so much from him already.

As though I had summoned him with my thoughts, Kabir came out of the bedroom to join us once more and seemed to read the expression on my face at once. He frowned.

"Everything alright?" he asked, and Rashi twisted around so she could speak directly to her brother.

"Yes, it's all great," she replied. "We've actually just had a spot open up at the shelter, so Aamna's going to come down and join us tomorrow evening."

"Oh," he managed in response, and I couldn't read the tone of the noise he made. Was he glad that I was going? Relieved? Upset?

"I can't stay long; I have to get everything ready back at the shelter for you." Rashi got to her feet. "But I wanted to come and give you the good news in person."

"Thank you," I mumbled, on autopilot, and she squeezed my shoulder.

"We're looking forward to having you," she told me, and she went to speak with Kabir for a moment and left me on the couch. Their voices faded out to nothingness in my ears, as I was so focused on the rush of thoughts running through my brain. He was just a man, and no matter how strongly I felt for him, I couldn't expect him to fix me. Not when there was a whole shelter out there to help me do just that.

Rashi said goodbye to the two of us and left, and Kabir stood behind me, breathing heavily. I wanted to turn around, to beg him to let me stay, but I had made my decision. I was going. It was the best thing for both of us. Even if I couldn't shake the fear at the back of my mind that he would forget about me, just like all those men who had used me and left me.

"So, you're leaving?" he asked finally, his voice quiet. I nodded.

"This was always meant to be temporary, wasn't it?" I turned to him, hoping that somehow he would see through my game and understand that I wanted nothing more than to stay with him. But that was foolish. He couldn't read my mind. Maybe he was glad that I was going and he didn't have to put up with a houseguest for much longer.

"Of course," he nodded, and he turned towards his office. "I have some emails to respond to, if you'll excuse me."

I watched him leave, and then sank into the couch and hugged my arms around myself. I took in this place one more time, knowing that today could be the last day I spent here. I closed my eyes and lay back on the couch, as though I could get it to absorb me, so I would never have to go.

Kabir avoided me for most of that day, and it was like the spell that we had cast together the night before had been broken. I was leaving, and he was keeping me at arm's length for reasons I couldn't imagine. His cook came by that evening and made us some dinner. I wanted to take a little of it to Kabir, but that would have been too painful. I knew that any little scrap of intimacy I allowed myself to feel for him was only going to make it harder to pull myself away, and I had made my decision to leave. I ate on the couch, staring at the blank TV, wishing I could just rewind to the night before, when we had been watching that movie together and had finally given in to one another.

I washed and brushed my teeth, and went straight to my bedroom. I was physically tired, but my brain felt as though it was pulsing with neon for all the sleep I was going to be able to get. I wanted to be with him, to fall asleep in his arms, knowing that we could spend the next day together, and the one after that, and the one after that.

I stared at the spot on the ceiling that I had become intimately familiar with during the nights that I had stayed here, sleepless. I kept on telling myself it was for the best. I mean, this house he lived in, the life that he lived, it was so distant and different from anything I had ever known, even before I was taken. He was suited to some woman who was easy, classy, from a good family, who didn't come with years of traumatic baggage for him to work through. He might have liked me now, but how much would he like me when I had a panic attack at a family event? When I couldn't come to his work party because I was too scared of the thought of being around that many men at once? When I woke up in the night, trembling and shaking, panicked at the memory of being raped, over and over again? I didn't want to feel this way, but I did, and I knew it wasn't his burden to bear. It was mine, and mine alone.

As I lay there in the dark, I heard footsteps. At first, I thought he was going to the bathroom, but then he came to a halt in front of my door and didn't move for a moment. My heart was pounding, and with every bit of psychic energy that I could muster, I willed him to come inside. To my delight, I heard the door handle go, and I sat up to watch him slip into my room.

"Aamna?" he asked softly. I could barely make him out in the dimness of the night, but I didn't care.

"I'm awake," I told him, and he came and sat on the edge of the bed, a reflection of what he had done that morning.

"I can go if you want," he replied, and I shook my head. I reached out to touch the inside of his wrist, that point where I could feel the blood pulsing through his veins.

"Stay," I murmured, and he looked at me for a moment, as though arguing the point inside his own head. And then, giving in, he slipped down on the bed and snuggled against me, wrapping his arms around me from behind. I knew that this was only going to make it harder to pull away from him when the time came, but I didn't care. I wanted him here, with me. I never wanted this to end. I was falling for this man, and the thought of pulling away from him hurt me in a way I never thought was possible. I had spent the last few years trying to escape from men, and now the one I wanted to stand by, I had to leave. It didn't feel fair.

But it was right. And, if everything fell into place, maybe he would wait for me. Maybe I could come back here, and we could pick up where we left off. Perhaps I could come back when I had formed myself into the kind of woman he deserved to be with. And, as I felt his breath steady and slow against me as he fell into sleep, I vowed to myself I would find a way to come back here, to be with him. Because the thought of leaving this behind for good made my heart hurt.

7

Kabir

I could feel the weight of her in my arms when I woke up – that was all I could focus on for a moment, and it was enough to get me to forget that she would be leaving later that day. For a blissful second, I existed in a space beyond reality, where the two of us could actually be together, where I didn't have to worry about her leaving me.

But then I opened my eyes and saw her lying there, and remembered that she was due to leave in just a few hours. I held her close, closing my eyes and willing myself back to sleep, so I didn't have to face up to the day, but it was too late. I was awake. I rested my head against her shoulder, not wanting to pull away just yet.

"Kabir?" her voice surprised me. I pulled back to look at her and saw that her eyes were already open.

"Aamna," I quickly lifted myself out of bed and got to my feet. Any moment I spent here with her, any second longer, it was just going to make things harder when it would be the time for her to leave for real.

"Are you alright?" she asked quietly, and I instantly felt a twist of guilt for acting so off with her. She didn't know that I was protecting myself. As far as she was concerned, I had just switched from the honeymoon phase to a jerk over the course of a day, and there was no good reason for it. I sat back down on the bed next to her and reached out to take her hand. Yes, it was only going to make parting more painful, but I wasn't going to let her leave thinking I felt anything but good things for her.

"I'm fine," I promised her. "Just thinking about what you need to do today."

"How about we have some breakfast, and we can go out and pick up whatever you need for the shelter?" I suggested, to which her face lit up.

"That sounds great," she agreed, her teeth resting on her bottom lip for the briefest moment as she looked at me. And I felt that warmth in my stomach that builds of desire for her. But I knew I had to face up to reality sooner or later, and making love to her again was only going to render that harder; nearly impossible.

She slid out of bed and headed through to the bathroom to get ready, and my gaze was drawn to her feet – no, her ankle, that thin loop of metal resting around her skin. It was one of the first things I'd noticed about her, so delicate and tempting. I got to my feet once more, this time on the way to the kitchen so I could grab something for the two of us for breakfast. She was going to have a long day ahead of her, and the least I could do was make sure she was well-fed.

As I laid out some food for breakfast, the way I had done the morning before, I was alone with my thoughts once more and found my mind drifting back to the last few weeks in her company. I had never believed that my feelings for someone could grow so sharply. It was strange to think that a mere month prior to this I had no idea who she even was, and now the thought of her leaving felt like a knife twisting deep into my gut. I had worked so hard to make sure my life was chaos-proof, to keep my job going and my family happy and my home comfortable, and now this woman had dropped into the middle of it and made me question everything that I had been so certain of before. I wondered if she knew the power she had over me.

She emerged from the bathroom, face cleaned, hair brushed and pulled back. She joined me at the counter. "What is it?" I asked her, and she cocked her head at me.

"I just can't believe this is the last day I get to spend with you," she confessed, and I felt that knife twist deeper into my gut.

"You heard what Rashi said," I reminded her, as much reiterating the point to myself as to Aamna. "It's the best way for you to get better. I can't give you everything they can down there."

"I know," Aamna agreed. "But I just—"

Whatever she had been planning on saying, she stopped herself dead in her tracks, silencing herself swiftly and sharply. I knew how she felt. It was as though I didn't trust myself to say anything other than careful repetitions of the points that Rashi had made the day before, as though I would do something stupid, like declare my love for her and beg her to stay, if I let my mouth run away with me.

"I'll call my driver to take us into the city center," I told her. "Then we can pick up whatever you need."

"You don't want anything to eat?" she asked, and I shook my head.

"I'm not hungry," I replied. It was the truth. My stomach was grinding with the stress, with the fear of saying goodbye to her. Of what it might mean if I couldn't let go so easily.

I called up the driver and carefully, slowly got ready in the bathroom. This was the last image she was going to have of me for a long time, and I wanted it to be a good one.

When I emerged from the bathroom once more, she was still sipping on her coffee – and she raised her eyebrows when she laid eyes on me.

"Wow," she grinned, her gaze flicking up and down my body. "You look…"

She got off the chair, padding in her bare feet towards me, the anklet clinking slightly as she moved. She slipped her hands around my neck, and for a moment I thought she was going to kiss me, as though she was going to beg me to stay. I looked deep into her eyes and smiled down at her, ready to accept at once. But then, I realized she was fixing my collar, making it straight against my neck. Then she withdrew her hands and the moment was gone.

"There," she stepped back, satisfied. "You look very handsome."

I thought I heard the faintest hint of a wobble in her voice, and some part of me wanted to press a little further to find out where that came from, but downstairs my driver had arrived, and I knew we had to get going.

I took Aamna down to the car that was waiting for us outside, and she slipped into the back seat and leaned against the plush leather, smiling.

"I can't remember the last time I was in a car this fancy," she remarked with a fluttering smile as I joined her in the back, after giving the driver our destination.

"Well, that means you won't soon forget this one, huh?" I shot back playfully, and she reached over and touched my hand as she laughed. The contact, however brief, was electric. I felt as though she had sent a jolt through my whole system. I withdrew my hand without thinking, knowing that this was going to be hard enough as it was. Her smile curled down at the corners, and I felt instantly awful for making her feel that way.

"Sorry," I shook my head. "My hands are cold. I don't want yours getting that way as well."

She turned to look out the window and watched as the streets whipped by in front of her. I noticed that her breathing was getting a little shallower as we headed for the centre of the city.

"Are you alright?" I asked softly, and she glanced over at me and nodded.

"I'll be alright," she promised me. "It's just that I haven't been this far into the city since… since, you know, since they found me. It just reminds me of all of it, that's all."

I wanted to curse myself out. How could I have been so stupid? I should have taken her somewhere else, somewhere that she wouldn't be dragged back into those dark memories that lived inside her.

"We can go somewhere else," I suggested, "Anywhere. You name the place."

"Back in time, so none of this ever happened?" she suggested with a wry smile, and then she shook her head and continued, "No, really. It's alright. I have to get used to being in the city again, I can't avoid it for the rest of my life."

We arrived at the shopping centre. She was instantly pinned close to my side, looping her arm through mine and clutching it tightly as we made our way into the large, modern building. To anyone passing by, we must have looked like any other regular couple. The thought made me happy, even though it couldn't have been further from the truth.

"So, what do you need?" I asked her, and she shook her head and raised her eyebrows.

"You've already been so generous with me, I don't want to exploit that," she replied.

"I just want you to be comfortable when you go to the shelter," I told her firmly. "Anything you think would make it easier, tell me."

"Come on; let's start with some new clothes, huh?" I suggested, and she managed a smile and nodded.

"That sounds like a good start," she agreed, and we ducked into the shop closest to the entrance, one that offered a range of sleek, modern clothes for women like her.

We spent most of the afternoon going in and out of stores and shops and chains until we had everything that she could possibly need to start a new life – clothes, toiletries, make-up, books. She loved the books the most and spent a long time tracing her fingers over the spines of the novels in the adult fiction section of the bookstore before coming to rest on a handful that she knew she would read.

"I used to love reading so much." She sighed, as we paid for the books and I took the bag for her. "I can't remember the last time I just sat and read a book in one sitting. I love it so much."

"Well, now you've got plenty to keep you busy." I grinned at her, and she bumped her hip against mine playfully as we made our way out of the shop.

"Yeah, I think Rashi's going to have a hard time getting my nose out of those things," she admitted, and I laughed.

"Oh, my sister has her ways," I wiggled my fingers in play-mysteriousness, and she linked her arm through mine once more. I felt that same twinge in the bottom of my stomach, the one that said that this was right, that us being together made sense. I ignored it once more. I had to support her in doing the right thing, even if it meant being away from me.

"Anything else you can think of?" I asked her quickly, glancing at my watch. Rashi had said someone would come by to pick her up in the evening, so I only had a matter of hours left with her at this point. The thought made my head hurt.

"Unless you want to buy me the house to put all this stuff in, I think we're good," she teased. "Thank you for all this, Kabir. Really. I don't know what I'd have done without you…"

"It's just stuff," I shrugged. "I can spare the money. It makes no difference to me."

"No, not just the things," she shook her head. "More than that. These last few weeks, I never thought I…"

She trailed off, and for a moment I thought she was just searching for the right words. And then I saw her eyes lock on to something behind us, and her face drained to almost deathly pale. Her arm slipped from mine, her whole body going limp.

"Aamna?" I went to touch her hand, but she pulled it away from me. She was still staring at something in the distance. I twisted around to try and catch a look at it, but just found myself faced by the bustling crowds of weekend shoppers. I couldn't see anything there that could have frightened her. And yet, when I turned back to her, she looked as though she was going to pass out.

Her legs began trembling, and I quickly darted towards her and wrapped my arms around her, keeping her from going crashing into the ground. She clutched on to me, her fingers sinking into my back, as though she was hanging on for dear life.

"We need to get out of here," she mumbled in my ear, her voice taut and tense. "Now."

"Aamna, what's going—"

"I'll tell you when we're back in the car," she promised me. "I just need to get out of here. Please, Kabir."

I could hear the fear in her voice, could feel the tension written all over her body, and I knew she wasn't kidding. With my arm around her waist, I manoeuvred us to the front of the mall once more, where the driver was still waiting for us. I hurried her to the car, and she practically dived into the backseat, cowering against the far window. I quickly loaded up the bags and joined her.

"Back home, please," I leaned forward and gave the driver his orders, and we drove away swiftly. She pushed herself up on the seat, peering back at the mall, as though she was convinced that whatever had scared her so much was coming after us right there and then.

"Aamna, you need to tell me what's going on," I told her, and she turned her gaze back to mine. Her eyes were glazed over, as though she was in another place entirely. She closed them for a moment, took a deep, shaky breath, and then looked at me once more. This time, she seemed more focused, even though I could still feel the nervous energy zipping around her body, like she was on a countdown timer to explosion.

"I saw him in there," she told me, her head drooping down, the exhaustion taking her.

"Who? Who did you see?" I turned around, wondering if I could catch a glimpse of whoever it was who had terrified her so deeply. She shook her head, and I realized there were tears dripping down her face.

"The man who…" She shook her head again and started over. "Shekhar, the man who used me."

I fell silent. A swell of rage hit me, so intense it made my head spin, and some stupid part of me wanted to turn the car around, find this man, and let him know exactly what I thought of him. But I knew that wouldn't help her right now; she didn't need my anger piled on top of everything else. She needed me to take some of her pain, to carry it for her a while.

"Your pimp?" I asked gently, and she nodded. I hadn't seen anything, but that didn't mean she was wrong. Maybe her brain had conjured the image and forced her to re-live it. It didn't matter. She needed my support, and that was all that mattered.

"He... he was the one who ran the place," she continued, the words tumbling out of her as though she didn't know how to stop them. "I was so scared of him. But he took a liking to me. He thought... he told me..."

She gasped for breath and buried her face in her hands, and fell silent once more. I reached over and held her again. I could feel her entire body trembling in my arms, as though she had been set to vibrate. I closed my eyes and ignored the anger in my system, focusing that energy on taking care of her instead. She needed me. And if I ever got the chance with that guy again, I would kill him with my bare hands.

We arrived back at the villa. Aamna was practically comatose on the seat, not crying anymore, but just staring off into space like all those dark memories were running through her brain like an awful movie. I scooped her into my arms, and she nestled against my chest as I carried her to the house.

I laid her down gently on the couch and kneeled before her; she took a deep breath and opened her eyes, focusing them on me once more.

"I can't go to the shelter tonight," she told me, her voice tiny. "I can't go. I can't leave this place. I can't leave—"

"Let me call Rashi," I told her. "Give me five minutes. I'm sure she'll understand."

I quickly stepped out of the room and called my sister.

"Kabir?" Rashi answered the phone. "Everything alright?"

"Everything's—" I almost replied in the affirmative on instinct, but I stopped myself at the last second.

"Aamna thinks she saw someone at the mall," I told her, lowering my voice. "Her ex-pimp?"

"Oh," Rashi sounded surprised. And then she changed her tune. "*Oh.*"

"What's going on?" I asked urgently.

"One of the girls at the shelter saw some guy hanging around the place," she remarked. "Looked shifty, but she didn't recognize him. Apparently, he was there all afternoon earlier this week."

"You think it might have been him?" I asked.

"I have no idea." She sighed, the rush of static filling my ear. "But take care of her, alright? It could just be her paranoia, but still. She's going to need your support."

"I want her to stay here with me," I told her firmly. "I don't think she's up to going back to the shelter, not yet. Especially not if there's some guy there stalking around…"

"You really think it's the right thing?" Rashi asked fretfully, and I peeked inside to look over at the couch, where Aamna was still lying, limp as a ragdoll.

"I'm certain," I assured her, "I'll call you tomorrow, and we can take it from there, alright? But tonight, she just needs to be with me."

I finished up the call, stepping over the cluster of bags the driver had brought up for us a few minutes earlier. They seemed so strange now, a reminder of a time that had only just passed but felt like a million years ago. I joined Aamna on the couch once more and felt painfully impotent in the face of her agony. I had never dealt with something like this before in my life. But

I wanted her to be well, wanted her to feel safe here, and that meant stepping up and doing what I had to.

"Aamna, what do you want me to do?" I asked her gently. "Anything. Just tell me. What would make you feel better right now?"

"If that man was wiped off the face of the earth and I never had to think about him again?" she replied, snorting mirthlessly as she said it. "I'm sorry; I know you're trying to help…"

"It's alright," I assured her. "I understand. Hey, maybe I could run you a bath? You have all that new stuff to try out…"

"Actually, that sounds good." She nodded, managing to push herself upright. The tears had smudged some of her make-up down her face. I reached over and brushed away a smudge of black on her cheek. She leaned her head into my hand and smiled.

"I'm so glad you're here," she murmured, and I felt my heart swell once more. It was new to me, and I wasn't sure I would ever get used to how intense my feelings were for her.

I got to my feet and headed through to the bathroom to run her a bath. I came through to fetch her, offering her the soft, silky robe she had picked out from the store.

"Here," I handed it to her. "Take as long as you need. And if you want anything, you can just shout through, alright?"

"Alright," she agreed, and then she hesitated, crumpling the robe in her hand, and shook her head. "Kabir, I don't want to be away from you. When I saw him, I felt as though he was… I felt as though he was in me again; in my head. I don't think I can be alone right now."

I stared at her for a moment, not sure what she was asking for.

"What do you need?" I asked, and she bit her lip.

"Can you sit through there with me?" she replied, and I nodded at once. And then, an idea hit me.

"You go through and climb in," I told her. "I'll be there in a second."

She headed to the bathroom, and I went to grab one of the books we'd purchased earlier that day.

When I joined her in the bathroom, she was already in the bath. It was dark in there, but not so dark that I couldn't make out her face – drawn, nervous, her eyes darting back and forth even as I walked in. There were enough bubbles in the bath that I couldn't make out much of her body, except for the tops of her knees where she had drawn them into her chest. The scent of jasmine and rose filled the room, sweet and dark and spicy, like her, and I took up a spot on the outer edge of the tub beside her. She flicked a little splash of water on me, still playful, despite it all.

"I'm not sure if I can read that in here," she pointed to the book I was holding. "It's too dark."

"I thought I could read it to you," I replied, and a smile spread over her face. She leaned back on the edge of the bath and closed her eyes.

"That sounds perfect," she said, and I adjusted a few candles to make the space readable. I opened the book and began to read to her.

There was something shockingly intimate about that moment, and it took me a while to work out why. She had been rudely reminded of the worst things that had ever happened to her, in front of me. And, instead of running or hiding herself away, like a crab crawling back into its shell, she had told me the truth. She had let me help her. She had accepted my aid any way that I wanted to give it and that showed a trust that I wasn't sure even I had put in anyone else before.

I watched her face as I read to her, the sound of my voice filling the bathroom as I ran through the first chapter of the fantasy novel she had picked out. Slowly, a smile curled up onto her face, and softness took her being, as though she was letting go of what had just happened. I wanted nothing more than to slip into the bath with her, to hold her tight and let the water warm both of us together, but I knew that I had to let her set the pace when it came to that. She was so clearly shattered in so many ways, in ways I would never truly understand, and that meant I had to hold back where I could, no matter how much I wanted her.

I finished the chapter, and her eyes fluttered open once more.

"Thank you," she said. "That was… I feel so much better now…"

"It's alright if you don't," I told her gently. "You don't have to pretend with me."

She let her gaze lower once more and nodded.

"I think I need to go to bed," she admitted to me. "Is that alright? You don't mind?"

"Aamna, whatever you need, remember?" I reminded her. I got to my feet reluctantly, not wanting to leave her alone, but I knew I needed to give her the space. I headed out of the bathroom once more and glanced at the bags we'd purchased earlier that day.

I hung back for a moment and looked over at Aamna. I knew that I couldn't fix her with money or things, but only time and my care for her. And I knew, in that moment, that I was willing to do whatever it took to make that happen. I was here for Aamna, for good. No matter what happened. Nothing could stop me.

8

Aamna

I lay there in bed, listening to the slow breathing of the man next to me as he slept. No wonder he was tired. It had been a harrowing day. And I had been the one to bring it all on him.

It was all going so well until I saw Shekhar in that place. Sure, I had been sad at the thought of leaving Kabir and going to the shelter, but he seemed less cold than the day before, as though he was more open to the idea of reconnecting after I came back. And I saw it as a chance to make myself better for him – well, for myself too, but the incentive of being able to maintain a true, real relationship with Kabir was a better one. I felt hopeful, for the first time since I had heard the news that I would be going to the shelter the day before, and the day we had spent shopping together had been enough for me to convince myself that we were just an inch away from being a real couple.

I could still remember the exact moment I laid my eyes on Shekhar in that place. I would have known that face anywhere; I could have spent years trying to scrub it from my mind, and my gut would still have known that it was him. His face seemed to flicker in front of me, as though in the midst of a heat haze, like my brain was trying to convince me that he couldn't really be there. How foolish had I been to think I could leave it all behind, when I was still in the same city it all had happened?

I couldn't remember much after that – Kabir asking me what happened, him carrying me out of the car, Kabir calling Rashi to let her know that there was no way I could come to the shelter that night. All their voices sounded distant and removed, as though they were coming from another dimension. The panic was pulsing in my head, no matter how many times I told myself that I was safe, that Shekhar couldn't get to me here.

The first time I remember feeling like I truly inhabited my own body again was when I took that bath, and Kabir had read to me. I was sure I had wanted to be in his arms, but I knew that any touch right then would have sent me spiralling into the memories of all those touches I hadn't wanted before. His distance made me ache, but it was the right choice.

I slid into that robe, letting the soft, silky fabric wrap around me, and climbed into bed; he slid in next to me, and I moved against him, needing to feel his arms around me. I didn't want sex, and he seemed to understand that. I just needed him there, the promise of his safety, the knowledge that I no longer had to deal with Shekhar the way I used to.

He had fallen asleep quickly, but I had stayed awake for what felt like hours, staring into the muted darkness and wondering what the hell I was meant to do now. I could still feel Shekhar in my head, curling like smoke around my brain, blotting out all those things I knew for a fact: that Kabir took care of me, that he wanted me to stay. I wasn't worthy of a man like him. I wasn't sure if I ever had been.

Rashi had been right. He had already done so much for me. Sure, he had agreed to let me stay a little longer, but how long before he would find himself exhausted by all the help I needed, by all the kindness I required from him just to function? He was rich, handsome, kind, intelligent – he was the kind of man who would have had women lining up to be with him if he put himself out on the market. And here I was, sapping that energy, draining him of everything he had. When I looked at Kabir, I saw something so pure, so untouched by my past life, but it wasn't going to stay that way, not if I stuck around much longer.

He looked so much younger than he normally did. His face was peaceful and not weighed down by the stresses of the day. I wanted to keep him this way. I didn't want to sully him with my pain, with the weight of it. I reached over to stroke his hair gently, and he nestled further in against me, as though he could somehow sense what I was thinking and didn't want me to go. But he had no idea how bad it would get. We had barely scratched the surface of it today, and it had clearly exhausted him. I had been able to kid myself for a while that I would be able to bury down the nightmare I had been through, the trauma hidden from the world – but the incident today had undercut all of that. I couldn't hide. But I didn't have to drag him through it with me.

His phone buzzed on the table opposite us, and I hesitated for a moment before I reached for it. I knew I shouldn't have even picked it up, but he was fast asleep, and it could have been something important.

As soon as I saw the message waiting for him, I felt a flood of coldness move over my body. I stared at the words on the screen before me, and I knew that the sign I'd been waiting for was finally here.

'I know it's been a while since we broke up,' the text read. *'But I've changed, and I think you have too. I want to meet up with you again so we can talk. Chhaya:*'*

The message came from a number that wasn't saved on the phone, but it closed out with a kiss, a single one, as though the woman on the other end of the line was leaning through it to plant a kiss on the cheek of the man she wanted to see. I stared down at the message for a long time, longer than I should have, the words burning themselves into my brain as Kabir slept calmly beside me, oblivious to all of this.

This was it. The sign that I should just get out of there once and for all and never look back. Here was a woman, a woman he had dated before, reaching out to him and asking to see him once more. Whatever happened between the two of them, I had no doubt that she was better suited to him than I was. Everything that had happened that day had just underlined how broken I was, what I would be asking him to do by being with me. This woman, this Chhaya, she came to him willingly, not dumped on his doorstep because there were no rooms at the shelter. Why wouldn't he want that more than me?

I raised myself from the bed like a ghost, feeling as though I was moving through water. My limbs felt distant from my own form as I packed my things up as quietly as I could, gathering what I needed to in order to get out of here. I left most of the items he had purchased for me, so he could take them back to the store if he wanted, but I stuffed most of the books in my bag, unable to walk away from them.

I stood there, in the doorway of the room, and stared at him as he slept. Some part of me was silently urging him to wake up and stop me, but I had no idea what I would say if he did. I wanted to stay with him, but more than that, I wanted him to be free – free from the torment that I brought crashing down into his life, free from the trial of guiding me through real life in the real world. I might have been a project he could handle working on for now, but when the real world began seeping in once more, he would grow weary of me. I was simply making the choice for both of us, so that he wouldn't have to cast me out himself.

I stepped over to him softly in my bare feet and leaned down to plant a kiss on his temple. He shifted in his sleep and tilted his face up to mine, as though on the brink of speaking to me, but I pulled myself away before he could come out with so much as a word. Even if he had woken, I would have scuttled out before he could say anything to me. I lingered in the door for one more second, committing every inch of his face to memory. Then I grabbed the small bag I had packed and slung it over my shoulder.

I opened and closed the front door as quietly as I could, glad that all the staff members were off-duty so none of them could catch me in the act and ducked out into the overheated street below. I looked back and forth, trying to remember where I was in relation to anything else in the city. I would try to get to my parents' house. My heart swelled with the thought of it, though it stung for the thought of leaving Kabir behind. In a few months' time, he would have forgotten about me entirely, moved on to some woman who could give him what he needed, and I would have started my life anew without him. And that would be the best thing for both of us.

I would have to find a cab in the centre of the city and hope that my parents could pay for my fare when I arrived. It was impossible to keep the smile off my face as I thought about being with them again – I felt as though I had lived an entire life apart from them. I turned and began to stride with purpose down the street, away from the house, every step putting more and more distance between me and the man that I craved so deeply. But I kept my eyes focused forward; set my mouth into a hard line, told myself, over and over, that this was the best choice for the both of us, no matter how terrifying it was right now. He would wake up and thank me for what I had done; I had no doubt of that.

I hummed to myself, in time with the beat of my feet, a song that had embedded itself in my memory as a distant tune from long ago. I may have been walking away from Kabir, but I was walking there under my own steam, and that was more than I would ever—

When it came, it came so fast I hardly had time to feel scared – one hand across my mouth, and one hand around my waist, pulling me backward, like a magnetic force. I recognized those hands at once. My eyes widened as the panic kicked to life, and my last thought was of Kabir, sleeping in bed, as peaceful as a child, before my brain, trained to freeze, not fight, let my body go limp, and my mind go numb as I tried to block out what was happening all over again.

9

Kabir

I tore apart the house looking for her. Tipped up the couch, pulled the shower curtain across, ducked beneath counters, moved the beds out from the wall, as though she was some errant cat who could have hidden herself away in any of those places. The whole time, I was silently pleading with the universe for her to walk back through that door, confused at the state of the house, or to roll out of the corner of some bed I hadn't thought to check yet, a teasing smile on her face when she saw the mess I'd made of everything.

But she was gone. Utterly gone… Vanished in the night, as I slept. I would have feared her kidnap, but she had taken some of the books and packed a bag, so I knew she had to have left under her own volition; probably to go back to her family. Why would she want to be here with me when the people closest to her, the ones who likely didn't even know she was alive yet, were out there waiting for her?

I turned over the events of the day before in my head so many times that they felt like a wound I couldn't stop tearing open. What had I done wrong? What indication had I given to her that I didn't want her here? She had left, packed a bag and upped and walked out on me, and I had to accept that. The last thing she needed was to freeze with terror when she saw another man in the street, and I refused to do that to her. She had been in a delicate state when she had arrived here, and this kind of acting out had always been a possibility, so I just had to let go and move on.

That morning, I felt as though I had been run over by a train, my entire body flattened against the tracks as I tried to figure out what the hell I was meant to do next. It felt as though little reminders of her were lying around the house for me like bear traps, wide open and waiting for me to step in and get all caught up all over again. A hairbrush she had used, some of the clothes I'd brought for her; still strewn out on the bed, the remnants of the bubble bath she had used the night before. It took me hours to check my phone. Aamna had no need of my number before, given that we were living together, so I saw no reason to glance over the screen to see if she had sent me a message. When I did click it on, I raised my eyebrows when I saw what was waiting for me – a message from Chhaya. Now, there was a name I hadn't thought about in a while.

Three years since she had left me for someone else. We had dated for a long time, or what had felt like a long time. It was when we were both still in our early twenties – my mother had set us up. Chhaya's father, a wealthy old-money businessman, had worked with my father on a project and my parents had caught on to the fact that they had a single daughter. Most of my mother's attempts to hook me up with various people went far awry, but I still had to show willing and turn up in the first place. So, like usual, I did as I was told and took Chhaya out on a date.

Much to my surprise, we had actually hit it off. Or so I had thought. Our parents were very happy about our union. As per them, we were a match made in heaven, but a few months down the line I realized the truth of it. Basically, in the first year of our relationship, I had chased her like a hopeless romantic praying on the fact that one day she would stop being so cold and aloof towards me. That one day I would see her warmer side, her love, and kindness. At the age I was back then – stupid twenty-something – I believed that's all love was about. And I lavished her with my attention and garnered her with everything her heart desired.

But things never looked up with her. I still couldn't quite put my finger on the blur of bullshit that had gone down around the time our relationship had ended – she had met someone else or some crap around it. I didn't care much then; I don't care at all now. She had that way about her, those sharp edges and that hardness, that let me know she was capable of doing anything she set her mind to. And I didn't mean that in the kindest way I could. I remembered the day she had left me, standing in the doorway of her apartment and glaring down at me as though this was somehow all my fault.

"It didn't have to be like this," she declared dramatically. She was always dramatic, as though she was acting in a soap opera and was the only one in her life who knew it.

"But you're the one leaving me," I pointed out to her calmly.

"He understands me in ways you never could," she told me, clearly annoyed that I wasn't throwing myself down at her feet and begging her to stay.

"Then go be with him," I waved my hand. "I don't want to keep you from your one true love..."

And with that, she stormed out. I had half-expected her to come back a few days later, after things had failed with this new man and she wanted to crawl back into the comfort of what we had, but she didn't. And I found myself, not saddened by it, but feeling as though a weight had been lifted from my shoulders, as though I could move more freely than I had in a long time.

And that had been the last I'd heard of her, until that text. It seemed like some kind of fate, the day that Aamna left being the day that Chhaya reached out to me once again. Perhaps the universe was trying to tell me something, to guide me in a new direction. And who was I to challenge the will of the universe?

I fired a message back to her, agreeing to meet up with her – I had no intention of dating her once again, but seeing her would be enough to get my mind off what had happened, and perhaps I could make myself feel better. We could reminisce about old times – a time long before that woman with those pale eyes had walked into my house and left footprints all over my life. Besides, maybe she had changed – a lot had happened since we had last seen one another, and I knew for a fact that I was far removed from the man I had been back then. Perhaps the same was true for her.

I forced myself to go to work that day. I knew if I sat back at home, I would just brood about what had happened to Aamna. No matter how hard I tried to shake it, there was this feeling at the back of my mind, this certainty that something had gone wrong and that she was in danger. But I knew that wasn't the case. She wouldn't have had time to pack a bag of her favourite books and walk out of the villa if she had been under pressure from someone.

Chhaya and I exchanged a few messages over the course of the day. I did my best to be jovial and interested in what she was talking about, but it was nearly impossible. When she suggested that we meet for dinner, to catch up, I found myself agreeing without really thinking.

Chhaya suggested an expensive place in the centre of the city, and I agreed, knowing that she would expect me to pay for it, as she always had. I didn't mind. Perhaps it was for the best, to pour my time and energy into something that didn't feel like a black hole ebbing away everything inside of me.

I headed straight over there from work in the evening and arrived at the restaurant five minutes early. Chhaya was already waiting there for me. As I arrived, she rose to her feet from the table she had selected and moved towards me with a benevolent smile on her face, as though she was doing me a favour. She looked different than she had done the last time I'd seen her, for reasons I couldn't put my finger on – her face sharper, her features harder, as though something inside her had shifted from softness to steel.

"Kabir," she greeted me with a smile and planted a kiss on my cheek. "I'm so glad you could come."

"Me too," I replied, hoping that I sounded sincerer than how I felt. As she pulled away from me, I found myself staring down at her and replacing her briefly with Aamna in my head. I couldn't help but wonder what it would have been liked to take Aamna out like this instead, to show the world the woman I cared for so deeply, to have her on my arm.

Pushing those thoughts to the back of my mind, I focused on the evening ahead of me. Chhaya had made the effort to reach out to me and organize this, and the least I could do was focus my attention on her now.

"So..." She arched her fingers and pressed the tips together once we were sitting opposite each other. "It's been a long time, hasn't it?"

"Yeah," I agreed, and it felt like every word that came out of my mouth was an extraordinary effort. Chhaya eyed me, eyes deep brown and a little cold as she waited for me to say something else, and I flashed back to the first time I had laid eyes on Aamna, when those cool green orbs had gazed into mine and felt as though they had instantly taken up residence in my soul.

The waiter appeared with the bottle of wine we had ordered, and offered me a taste. I declined, pointing towards her, as she had been the one to order it.

"You're the man," she told me, voice a little hard. "You're meant to taste it first."

The waiter stood there, dithering between the two of us, clearly not sure what the right course of action was, as Chhaya looked at me expectantly. I smiled, assuming she was making a joke, and the waiter went to pour it into my glass as she had indicated.

"Mine, come on," she thrust her glass in his direction. "I was making a joke, for goodness sake, couldn't you tell?"

The waiter lowered his gaze apologetically and poured the wine into her glass instead, allowing her to taste it, and, finding it to her liking, pouring us both a glass. She eyed me over the top of hers, and I couldn't tell for the life of me what she was thinking about. I had never liked this side of her, the one that seemed to have such disdain for the people who ran through her day to make it easier.

"What have you been up to?" I offered hopefully, aiming to get her talking enough that she wouldn't notice my quietness. And, as she always did, she launched happily into a ten-minute spiel about herself, her life, how successful she'd been, how she'd left that terrible man who she had been with after me because he just didn't *understand* her, and how, lately, she had wondered more and more about me and had felt drawn to reach out once more.

"I've been thinking about you so much, Kabir," she confessed, sliding her hand across the table and grasping mine for a moment. I knew what her touch meant. I understood from the look in her eyes how she intended this to be taken, that this was the great climax to our meeting again, the moment she confessed that she had missed me, that she wanted me back. As she rested her fingers against mine and gazed at me in the dim light across the table, I knew that this was her attempt at the beginning of a seduction.

But all I could think as I looked back at her was that I wished Aamna could have been in her place instead. I hated myself for it, hated myself for cutting myself off from the world this way, but I couldn't deny it. I drew my hand away from hers, and I saw her mouth turn down into an almost comical frown. She opened her mouth to say something, and then closed it again, thinking better of it. Well, that was some development – the Chhaya I had known before would have given anyone denying her what she wanted a piece of her mind and stormed out, claiming she didn't even want it in the first place. Perhaps she had changed, after all.

"What about you?" she asked, letting her hand come back to rest on her lap, swiftly cooling the flash of irritation in her eyes to something more neutral. "What's been happening in your life since I left?"

And with that, I managed to come up with enough to keep the both of us distracted for the rest of the evening – the news of what had been happening at work, with my family, with the friends that we had shared back in the day. And I found the evening pleasant enough, a distraction from the roiling sea of discontent that was raging inside of me at that moment. I felt nothing for her anymore, but perhaps the two of us would work better as friends than we ever had as lovers.

When the evening ended, she leaned up to plant a kiss on my cheek, as she had done when she'd greeted me, and I reached down inside myself to feel for a hint of chemistry, a hint of attraction, anything that might indicate my heart was not yet totally broken. But as she pulled back and looked into my eyes, I stared back at her and knew it wasn't true.

"Thank you for a wonderful evening," she murmured, her voice laced with a sultry deepness that I knew was an extension of her seduction from earlier. "I'd love to do this again sometime."

"Sure," I agreed, not wanting to shoot her down quite yet.

"Soon?" She prompted. Her flirtations were familiar, but they did little to excite me. I took a deep breath and offered her a smile.

"Soon," I replied, and I turned to head to a cab to get back to my place. Though I would be alone there, but being alone with my memories of Aamna was better than forcing falseness in the hopes of moving on from her. And besides, for just the few minutes of this taxi ride, I could pretend that I was going to get back home and pull open the door and find her there, waiting for me, as she had been before, as I had hoped she always would be.

10

Aamna

When I snapped back to my body, it took me a moment to realize that I was no longer with Kabir, no longer in his villa, no longer safe. The bag of books that I had grabbed before leaving was the first thing that my eyes focused on. It was dumped in the corner with the books spread all over.

I was sitting on the edge of a bed, in a room I didn't recognize – small, the walls oppressive and peeling with old paint, the smell of damp circling around my head and feeling as though it was choking me out. I remembered the hand around my face, the other around my middle, and touched my ribs to find a shock of pain beneath my fingers. I was hurt. It had been a long time since I had felt this kind of pain, but the sensation of it on my body was familiar, like an old companion.

As soon as those hands had touched me, I had known who it was. I would have recognized them anywhere. I had recognized him when I had seen him at the mall, and I recognized his touch when his hands had circled around me to drag me back to the hell I had only just managed to claw my way out of in the first place.

But I wasn't back in the brothel, which was strange. I got to my feet, slowly, and hoped that this was all some bad dream, a memory forcing itself on me in a new way.

But then the door opened, and reality came crashing down on top of me like a tropical storm.

Shekhar stood there before me while a smile on his face, a smile that seemed dissonant to what was going on – as though he expected me to return it, to run into his arms and let him hold me there. I clenched my fists at my sides, the last vestiges of strength I had in me ready to fight.

"What am I doing here?" I asked him quietly. My voice around him dropped away to nothing, fearful of the retribution if I did something wrong, if I acted in any way that might anger him. His smile widened, and he spread his hands out in front of him as though handing me the sweetest gift he could imagine.

"I've brought you home," he told me, taking a step towards me. He was here before me again, his face seared itself on to my brain like a painful brand. Sharp eyes, a long, slightly hooked nose, skin mottled with the evidence of his heavy alcohol use. He was lean and thin, wiry, battle-ready, his body built not for aesthetics, but for violence. He looked like a monster, poured into a human form and bursting to get out of his shell.

"This isn't my home." I shook my head firmly. Never in my life had I talked back to him like this – not without paying for my words, at least – but I knew I shouldn't be here. I had tasted a tantalizing glance of the life that I could live, the life that he had nothing to do with. Now I had something to fight for.

"You were gone for so long," he shook his head, ignoring the words that had just come out of my mouth. "I didn't know what to think. And then I saw you, at that mall, and I just… I knew you had come to find me. I knew you were searching for me the same way I was searching for you."

He moved towards me again, and every nerve ending in my body was screaming at me to get away from him, to put as much space between the two of us as I could, but the room was small, and it felt as though with his every step, the walls were getting tighter in on us. I could feel my muscles tensing, my brain shutting off, my tongue growing heavy in my mouth, my body doing what it could to protect me from the violence, the horror of what he was planning to inflict on me.

He clasped my arms, but not so tightly that it appeared he was trying to hurt me. I would have preferred it if he was. At least then, I would know how to react to the situation; I would understand what he was doing to me. My mind was racing so fast I couldn't form a coherent thought for the life of me, staring at his face, trying to get a read on this situation.

"I missed you so much," he murmured, and his face softened, terrifyingly. The Shekhar that I knew kicked doors open, screamed at people three rooms away and filled the whole house with his rage. He always grabbed me by the arm and physically dragged me places when I wouldn't follow him at once. I could still remember, so vividly, the sight of him on top of me, the feeling as though I was watching my own body violated by him. Ice was running through my veins, my feet rooted to the spot like I would never move them again.

"What are you talking about?" I demanded, and finally, I found some reserve of strength somewhere inside of me and wrenched myself out of his grasp. His face dropped, but he let me move away from him. I scanned the room once more – no windows and the only door was the one he was standing before. I had no idea where I was in the city or if I was still even in Delhi. If I made a break for it, he would find me again fast enough, and this time, I doubted he would hold back on his anger.

He had never been good at that before. How many times had I heard him around that place, screaming, shouting, drunk, high, stuffing money into his pocket before he came to work out his tensions on one of the girls. He ran that place like a prison, stamping out anything that looked like dissent. I could still remember the first time he'd laid eyes on me, when he'd come to try me for the first time, sliding up in bed beside my curled form and running his hands over my body as though it was fresh meat.

"Aamna," he spoke my name, and I wanted to claw it out of his mouth, scrub it from his memory.

"What?" I spat back. Anger was roiling through my system like a forest fire, and I felt out-of-control.

"I know that I didn't treat you the right way when I first knew you," he looked at me with a soft smile, as though he truly believed that this would be enough to make amends for everything he had put me through.

"And when you left..." He hesitated, shaking his head. "I understood. I understood that I had always had these feelings for you and that I had been just trying to ignore them all this time—"

"Keep ignoring them," I muttered, not thinking before the words came out of my mouth. My muscles tensed, ready for pain, a punishment for my harshness. But he continued smiling at me, unwavering, as though he hadn't even heard me speak.

"Sometimes, it takes losing something to realize how much you need it," he replied calmly, and it was as though he'd gone and watched a bunch of romantic movies and was just lifting dialogues straight from there, in the hope that I would go swooning over him by design. But he couldn't just tell me things were different and have me believe it. He had wrecked my trust

– not just in him, but in everyone. Standing here before him now, I felt such anger that I could feel myself lifting from my own body, no room for my consciousness left in there with all that rage.

"How did you find me?" I demanded, and he shook his head.

"I just knew where you were going to be," he continued. "I let my senses guide me to you, and then, there you were. With a man, but I understand. I had to distract myself with other women, too."

Kabir… *Kabir…* He would have realized that I was gone by now, but he must have noticed that I'd packed a bag and gathered some books before I left. He probably would think I had abandoned him. And he wouldn't come looking for me. I closed my eyes and tried to find his mind in mine, find that connection, send a distress signal all the way down and along until I knew it had reached him…

"I started looking for you at the shelter," he began to pace back and forth.

"And I found some of the other girls there," he shook his head. "But I didn't want them back. I'm not sure any of them liked me, anyway."

I remembered how I had felt when I had laid eyes on him at the mall, the coursing, screeching panic that had overwhelmed me, and how those girls at the shelter must have felt the same thing seeing him again. Each of them met with the image of their own personal hell in human form. I hated that this man, this half-man, had so much power over all of us.

"After I lost everything," he continued, shaking his head again and smiling, as though he could barely believe he was telling this to me. "I changed, Aamna. I changed. I became someone else. I realize now… what I was doing; it was all to bring me to you. You've changed me, beyond anything I could ever have imagined…"

He gazed at me, his eyes expectant, and I could tell that he was waiting for me to shower him with praise, to accept this new form of Shekhar that he was so sure he had become. I wasn't sure how long I just stared at him for, but it felt like a lifetime. And no matter how hard I looked, all I could see in him was this human shell for the creature that had ruined my life, my sense of safety, my ability to give and accept love.

"I don't believe you," I replied bluntly and, to my surprise, the words felt good coming out of my mouth. I kept going.

"I don't believe you've changed at all," I told him, keeping my distance, even though I wanted nothing more than to punch him in the face and watch his certainty wither in front of me.

"Aamna, I don't know what it's going to take for you to understand that things are different," he continued, and I could really see that he believed this – somehow, when the brothel had been raided and ruined, he had slipped into some other mindset, one that would protect him from his failure which would have been fine, if I hadn't been the focus of it. He had shifted his obsession with keeping that place profitable on to me.

"There's nothing you could do," I snapped back. I had returned to my body, and I could feel the fury fizzing in my fingertips. I closed my eyes for the briefest moment and remembered how it felt to sleep next to Kabir, how safe it had been for me, how I had chosen it for myself. "The only thing that could make me believe you care for me at all…" I told him, my voice oddly calm, as though this was coming from a place of deep, utter certainty. "Is let me out of here and never come near me again."

I could see the blackness enter him again, like the spirit of something demonic. His shoulders tensed and he backed up, to fill the doorway, blocking my exit from this place. "I'm going to give you some space," he told me, his voice barbed, the words catching on my skin, tearing pieces. "And we can talk again later. You must be tired. Get some sleep."

"Let me out of here," I told him again, bluntly. "I don't want to be with you, Shekhar. I..."

I wanted to tell him that I hated him, that I would have never hated any being more on earth than him, but the blackness was consuming him, swallowing up anything that might have found mercy for me. He lifted his hand and slammed it down against the doorframe, hard enough that the whole thing rattled.

"Aamna!" he barked, the sound of my name slashing through the air. "I'm trying to make things right here. Why won't you let me?"

He moved towards me again, and this time it was with purpose, with those hands meant to hurt. I backed to the wall behind me, wanting to sink through and fade to nothingness, the only place he couldn't get me.

I didn't say a word to him, as though he was on a hair-trigger and the slightest thing would have been enough to set him off. All those memories that had only come to me in my dreams before were flooding my system, my body launched into protective mode, trying to mitigate the damage he could do to me. I had no idea how far he might go. "Sleep," he ordered me, and I knew there was no point arguing with him any further. He glared at me for another moment, and I didn't say a word, lips pressed together, hands flat to the wall behind.

"Sleep," he muttered again, and he turned and made his way out of the room. As soon as the door was shut behind him,

I hurried up to flick the lock across and then collapsed back against the wall. I clasped my hand over my mouth and sank to the ground. I was too frightened to cry. I felt as though I was sliding backwards, back to the person I had been before, the victim, the exploited, the used. I closed my eyes as tight as I could and clung to the thought of Kabir and the person I had been when I was with him.

11

Kabir

"How long are they going to make us wait for a table?" Chhaya demanded, tapping her foot against the floor and rolling her carefully made-up eyes at me. I managed to smile back at her, even though I wanted to roll my eyes right back.

"Well, if you'd booked a table for us—"

"We shouldn't have to book!" She exclaimed, throwing her arms in the air and attracting the attention of a couple of people waiting next to the host stand as well. "This is the kind of place that would be *glad* to have our patronage."

"Clearly not that glad," I muttered back without thinking, forgetting that Chhaya didn't exactly take well to being undermined.

"What did you say?" She planted her heel in the ground and swivelled around on it, as though she was wishing she could grind it into me instead.

"Nothing," I held my hands up. "Just hope they won't be much longer, that's all."

"We'll expire from hunger before we get a table," she sighed heavily, as though she really believed the words coming out of her mouth. "I can't believe this..."

I didn't bother to comment again, knowing it wasn't worth my while to delve into exactly why it was about the most entitled thing in the world for her to rock up at a restaurant that was practically the most in-demand in Delhi and expect them to cow to the two of us. I glanced around, and noticed a few people looking in our direction, probably wondering why she was making such a fuss. I was starting to wonder why I had even come on this date in the first place.

Well, no, I knew what I was doing here – I knew I was here because I wanted to do everything I could to get Aamna out of my head and, so far, sitting around getting mildly irritated by Chhaya was a far better option than sitting at home getting deeply annoyed by my inability to let go of the woman I wanted back. I still had no idea where she had gone to, but when I had told Rashi about the situation, she had told me to let things go.

"She's got family in the city," Rashi pointed out. "She probably went back there. This has all been a lot for her, Kabir; you've got to understand that. The way she reacts to things might not seem logical to you or me, but it does to her, and that's the most important thing."

"Right," I nodded, and I tried to ignore the twist in my stomach at the thought of her getting up and leaving in the night. Without even saying goodbye? It didn't feel right. But Rashi was the one who understood this far better than I ever could, and I wasn't going to push her to give me permission to put my life on hold and chase a woman who had left me.

"The two of you... you grew a little too attached to her," Rashi hesitated for a moment, trying to find the best way to phrase it

– even for her bluntness, she could tell that this had been hard on me. I knew what she was asking, but the thought of trying to quantify what Aamna and I had shared was painful, impossible, like trying to trap the galaxy in a glass jar.

"The two of us," I sighed and repeated after her. She nodded, her mouth tight. She reached over and patted my arm.

"I'm sorry," she murmured, and I didn't dare to look in her eyes for fear of spilling everything that I had been keeping so carefully to myself all this time.

When I had told her that Chhaya was back in my life, her eyes had rolled so hard to the back of her head that I had been sure they would end up stuck there. She had never been the biggest fan of my ex, but given how Chhaya was, I couldn't blame her.

This was the fifth time the two of us had gone out together in the last ten days. She was constantly pressing me to spend time together, even though she never actually seemed to have a good time when we were out. But I kept agreeing, certain that things would have changed enough that I would eventually break through her shell and find the real Chhaya inside.

What shocked me was that she hadn't changed since we had split up. It had been so long ago. I looked back on the person I was then and felt as though I barely knew who he was; but she still seemed well-acquainted with the person she'd been before.

"Finally," she groaned loudly as the host approached us and gestured to a small table that had just become free. I had suggested we should go somewhere smaller, quieter, so we could actually talk, but she had insisted on this hip, busy, expensive place. Along with everyone else in the city, it seemed.

She smiled at me, a smile that barely reached her eyes, and I looked back at the exact same woman I had dated so many years ago. How could she not have changed? Did she really just reach twenty-one and think 'well, that's all the development I need as a person?' It was almost fascinating, in its own way, and part of the reason I kept on finding myself back here opposite her, even though I knew nothing was going to happen between us.

"It's so nice to come out like this." She smiled at me, as though she hadn't just been on the brink of throwing a tantrum in the middle of this restaurant a few minutes before. I managed to smile back.

"What kind of food do they do here?" I asked as the waiter arrived with our menus and a bottle of water.

"No idea," she shrugged. "But I've heard it's good."

I winced when I took a look at the prices. Not that I couldn't afford them, but I knew she would expect me to pay for her dinner, as well. And she never seemed to hold back on ordering the most expensive things on the menu. Now, that was something that had changed about her. Back in the day, she had always been keen to flash her cash around any chance she got, making sure that anyone paying attention could tell that she was from a well-off family and could afford anything she wanted. Maybe she had just realized that most grown men would lavish her with any kind of attention she wanted, and she no longer had to bother going into her own pocket for things?

"Hmm..." She closed the menu and leaned back in her seat. "You know, I'm not sure I like the look of this place after all. Everything on the menu looks so.... *fusion-y.*"

I stared at her, utterly incredulous, across the table.

"We just waited forty-five minutes for a seat," I remarked.

"But I just don't *want* to be here," she whined, and that wheedling tone was like a sense memory that shot me straight back to the dozens of dates we'd been on just like this when I had been young enough to think that her selfishness was cute and bold instead of seeing it for what it was.

"Fine," I got to my feet. "I know somewhere back in the city. Let's go."

I took her to a small place not far from my villa, glad to have some good food in my belly; it made it a lot easier to listen to her moaning about every little thing, including the décor and the way it smelled in there. As she nibbled on some of the dishes in front of us, I couldn't help but stare at her, searching for whatever it was I had seen in her back then. It was baffling to me, utterly and completely.

She insisted on riding with me back to the villa, tucking her arm through mine as we stepped out of the restaurant, and I waited to feel that spark of attraction, something, anything. No matter how I felt about her, Chhaya was an undeniably attractive woman, and any other man would have been thrilled by her touch. But I found myself cold towards her.

"I had such a wonderful time tonight," Chhaya fluttered her lashes at me pointedly, and it felt like she was doing what she knew she had to in order to seduce me. Even she didn't seem to really believe it, rather churning out the lines and the actions she knew were meant to lead to something happening. I couldn't figure out why she had been so insistent on us spending so much time together. Maybe she wanted to settle down and couldn't be bothered building a history with someone else, so just decided to tap into one she already had? Even still, she must have seen how awkward it was, how little we had to say to one another. I was swiftly running out of patience for it, and I was meant to be the one distracting myself.

She climbed out of the car with me, taking me by surprise – did she expect to be invited in? I paused by the door as the cab drove off, not sure how to get rid of her without being harsh.

"Kabir, I didn't realize how much I'd missed you until you were gone," she murmured, suddenly shifting towards me so that our bodies were mere inches apart. I had to tell her the truth, that this had been a mistake and that I had been wrong to lead her on like this. I let out a long sigh, shook my head, and opened my mouth—

But before I could say a word, she leaned up and kissed me. Hard. Her tongue was in my mouth at once, her hands clasping my head as though she knew I would try to get away, and it took me a split second to realize what was happening before I struggled to remove her. Grabbing her waist, I pulled her away from me, and the heat of her mouth on mine felt as though it was pulsing in a regular beat: *Aamna, Aamna, Aamna.* My heart ached in my chest. Now, the last woman to kiss me was Chhaya. Not the woman I wanted.

"What's wrong?" Chhaya furrowed her brow and then smiled at me seductively. "We can go upstairs if you don't want to start down here…"

"No, it's not that," I shook my head. "Chhaya, I'm sorry, but this isn't working out. I don't think we should see each other anymore."

"What?" Her voice rose into a sharp shriek, and I withered internally. The last thing I needed was a confrontation. I just wanted her to leave.

"I'm sorry, I shouldn't have led you on," I conceded. "But I don't think it would be good for either of us to start things back up. It didn't work then, and it won't work now."

She stared up at me, her mouth hanging open, looking like a cartoon character miming 'shocked'. How could she be surprised by this?

"You just haven't given me a chance," she fired back, furious. "You still think you're so above me just because I made some mistakes when we were first dating. You don't get to judge people on who they used to be, Kabir!"

I just stared down at her. I was gobsmacked. Had she really been under the impression that we had been having an amazing time this last couple of weeks? That the tension had not been building to near-unbearable levels?

"Listen to me," she grabbed my hand, and I drew it back without thinking. Her touch felt poisonous, like she was shooting venom into my system with every touch.

"Listen to me!" She exclaimed again, and I knew by now that the neighbours would be gathering at their windows, trying to figure out where all this commotion was coming from. I glanced around, hoping that I would be able to get this over with quickly.

"You're not even looking at me," she pointed out, shaking her head. "I mean, you can't even look me in the eye and tell me you don't want to be with me. I don't know what's going on, Kabir, but we're allowed to be together. You're allowed to want me..."

She moved towards me again, back in seduction mode, and I stepped back.

"I don't know how I can make this more obvious to you," I told her firmly. "I don't want this to happen. Any of it. I think you need to move on."

"I don't want to!" She exploded, and she seemed an inch away from stamping her foot on the ground like a child who wasn't getting her way.

"You don't get to make that choice," I replied, trying to keep my voice calm in the face of her overreaction. "Take some time to think about this. I don't think you want this, either."

"You don't get to tell me what I want," she jabbed a finger into my chest, hard. "*You* need to think about what's right for *you*.

You're not getting any younger, Kabir, and women are starting to talk – you're not married, you're not dating, you're not starting a family, what are you going to do with the rest of your life?"

As I looked down at her, her words sinking into my brain as I tried to make sense of them, a silent answer filled my head – Aamna. I knew I couldn't tell her about that, or any of what had happened between me and Aamna, but everything she had accused me of hiding from – I did want it, just not with her. With a woman who had left me without looking back. A woman I hadn't heard from in two weeks.

I looked her dead in the eye, no longer entertained by her antics. I wanted her gone.

"You should go," I told her firmly, and I saw her recoil slightly, surprised by my firmness.

"Fine," she tugged her jacket around her shoulders. "But I'll be here when you finally figure out that you need me."

"Alright," I shook my head and sighed as she turned and went to flag down a cab. I waited to make sure she'd found one alright, and then retreated to the villa. Instead of going to my bedroom, though, I found myself lingering in the doorway of Aamna's room. Staring at the muddled sheets, untouched from the morning I had woken up with her. I knew there was no way I was getting any sleep that night. Not without her at my side.

12

Aamna

I stared at the ceiling, at the peeling paint above me, and wondered how I had ended up here once more.

I lifted my head from the lumpy pillow and looked around, brow furrowed. I hadn't gone anywhere. I was still trapped here, cruelly ripped away from the life I had only caught a single glimpse of.

That small beautiful life with Kabir was the hardest part. If Shekhar had just taken me straight from *that* awful place to *this* awful place, I might have been more amenable. Maybe, just maybe, I would have gone along with it, have had convinced myself that it was so much better than what I had been forced to endure before so it *must* be romantic. But I had seen what life could have been like if I had just stayed with Kabir, if I had found the nerve in myself to accept that I was worthy of his affections and the life he brought with him. And that just made this so much harder to handle.

I wasn't sure how long it had been since Shekhar had taken me. A week, maybe more? The days seemed to blur into one another, as I spent most of my time sleeping to avoid him, pulling the covers up over my head and squeezing my eyes shut until I slipped into unconsciousness. Not that my sleep had stopped him before, but for some reason, he was approaching me a little differently now – as though he was willing to give me some space, some time. Not that much space, of course, as he still had me stuck in this dingy apartment, but he was treating me like I was an errant lover more than the exploited teenager he had dragged into his awful place and beaten and raped for years.

I couldn't have felt less for him – well, anything less than the utter disdain that filled my system every time I looked at him – but he seemed to adore me, carefully lying next to me while I pretended to sleep and stroking my hair, growing furious every time I would suggest leaving. For Shekhar, this was love or the closest thing he had known to it. And I had no idea why I was the focus of his attention.

No, that wasn't true. I was beginning to understand why I was here. When he had lost the brothel, his entire life had been torn away from him, everything that had given him power and control vanishing in a second without a moment's notice. When he had fled that place, he had told, he had been helpless:

"I've never felt that way in my life, Aamna," he spoke, reaching out to touch my face gently. His fingers were clammy on my skin, and I fought the urge to jerk away, knowing that his tenderness could morph to hard edges if I made the wrong move. I sat there, not saying a word, looking at him and waiting for him to continue.

"So powerless," he shook his head, finally letting his hand drop from my face. "And I thought… I tried to remember the last time I'd felt powerful without the old home, you know?"

He called it 'the old home', as though it had been anything other than a brothel that he had used to exploit innocent women like me. Shekhar refused to see the evil in what he had done, and sometimes I wanted to catch him by the shoulders and scream it into his face. Did he really believe he had done nothing wrong? Was he that sick? How much did a man have to move from his morals to sit there and talk as though years of violently exploiting women had been home for them? I swallowed my words, as I had done a dozen times over the course of the last few days, and waited for him to continue.

"And I thought of you," he reached out to take my hand, and I looked down at his fingers touching mine. I could physically see that our skin was in contact, but it was like I had floated from my body and couldn't feel it at all. I looked him in the eyes, pleading for some distant human part of him to see how much I craved my freedom, but I came up a dead blank. He really thought this was romance. That his feelings of power had come from love, not from the literal dominion he had held over me. "You always made me feel so strong, Aamna," he continued. "And I'm so glad we're finally back together…"

I had tuned out of the conversation then, as I often did when he began to profess his love for me. Usually, I just kept quiet and let him speak, and found that that seemed to satisfy him well enough. He didn't actually seem to want me to love him back, just to hear that he loved me, endlessly and without fail, as though that love would parlay itself into his redemption. As though anything he felt for me was close to love…

At least he had refrained from raping me for the time being. I supposed that it would rather break his fantasies of love and mutual adoration if he had to pin me to the bed like he had done before to have his way. He seemed set on seducing me, no matter how many times I bluntly turned down his advances. Every time he laid a hand on me, I felt as though I wanted to crawl out of my own skin, leave my body behind for him to do with what he wanted while my brain floated somewhere else, somewhere blissful, somewhere far from this.

Back with Kabir and the safety of his arms. That was where I wanted to go. As I stared at the ceiling above me, I willed myself back into that bed with him, before I had made the choice to leave him behind. I had been so convinced I didn't deserve that life, the one that he was offering me. I was so sure he deserved a better girl, someone like the one who had texted him. Maybe this was where I belonged, and everything that had happened with Kabir had been a break from reality, not the start of it. He hadn't come looking for me, or if he had, hadn't done a very good job finding me.

And what were the chances that I would get saved twice? I had had my chance to get out of this awful business, out of Shekhar's grasp, and I had been so scared by it that I'd ended up running away from my chance. It wasn't like they had a whole brothel to track now. It was just me and Shekhar in this dingy little apartment. Why would they think of looking for me this time? They had probably assumed that I had just decided to flee to somewhere on my own accord, to strike out in the world alone. And they were good people, so they would let me.

Rashi was so nice to me. On that first night, when she had taken me out of that place and bundled me into the back of her car and promised me that she would do everything she could do to take care of me in the face of what I had been through. I had felt numb against the cold evening air, unable to believe the truth. I was so certain that it was a trick and I would end back in the brothel sooner rather than later. And, well, I had managed to make that happen. Fleeing out on to the street in the middle of the night, it was like I had been running back into the arms of my old life, letting it hook its dark fingers around me and draw me back in once more.

I heard Shekhar at the door, pacing back and forth, probably trying to listen to see if I was awake. God knows what he wanted from me this time.

This time as he pushed the door open slowly to check if I was awake, I felt a swell of resolve. Kabir was fresh in my mind, his hands caressing my hair, his mouth covering mine, our bodies meeting and wrapping around each other like roots winding in the earth. Every time Shekhar touched me, it pushed those memories a little further back, making it a little harder for me to find them again.

I lifted my head to look at him as he entered. I had barely moved all day – maybe if I stayed so indolent, I would gain weight, and he would be disgusted by me. I would have done anything if it meant guaranteeing his rejection. I had managed to keep him at bay with excuses till now, but at that moment, I felt a swell of anger at the thought of the life he was keeping me from. I wanted to put up a fight. I wanted to make it hard for him.

"Aamna?" He asked quietly, moving towards me and perching on the end of the bed. I whipped my knees up to my chest, pulling away from him, putting as much space between us as I could manage.

"Leave me alone," I told him, voice hard. I didn't look at him, but I could feel his body stiffen as I spoke.

"Aamna, I just want to talk to you," he reached out to take my hand, and I pulled it away. Glaring off into space, I dared him to say another word to me. I wanted to reject him. I wanted to prove to him and to myself that there was nothing here and that I was bold enough to admit it.

"I don't want to talk," I replied.

"Are you tired?" He offered, clearly hoping that there was some reasoning behind my harshness. I shook my head.

"I just want to be left alone," I shot back, speaking each word as clearly and calmly as I could. My body was trembling – this kind of bluntness could only end badly for me, and yet, I felt as though the worst had already happened. There was nothing he could take from me that he hadn't already taken. I had nothing left to lose.

He let out a long sigh, and I could tell that he was frustrated by my lack of willingness. He was set on convincing me that he was a changed man, that things were different now and that I could trust him. And I could use that to my advantage. Every time I pressed him, pushed him, I could feel that hot flash of anger running through his body, the overheated blood in his veins yearning to do me harm, but he held back. I had no idea how long that would last for, but I planned to exploit it as long as I could.

"Fine," he got to his feet slowly, as though giving me the chance to concede and speak with him. "Get some sleep, if that's what you need so badly."

And with that, he turned and walked out of the room, leaving me there alone once more. A pulse of victory at what I had just done faded into a grey ball of grief as I realized that no matter how many times I turned him down, how many times I pushed him away, I would still be trapped here. I tucked my hand beneath my head and stared at the wall, imagining a window appearing in it, a window that looked out onto the street below, where Kabir was waiting for me. And for a moment it was so real I could almost feel it, and I found a smile curling up my lips, my mind soothed for an instant – until I heard a loud metallic crash from next door, and came jolting back to reality.

"Fuck!"

I heard Shekhar shout from the next room, and squeezed my eyes shut once more. He was angry. It was the first time I had really seen that familiar fury in him since I had been brought to this place, and I recognized it at once, the harshness in his tone, and the indiscriminate rage in his actions. I heard another crash, what sounded like a pan being hurled to the floor, and I did everything I could to pretend that it wasn't happening. As I lay there in bed, I focused on picturing a life far removed from this one, a life that was so close I could almost taste it. I hoped that one day it would be real again.

13

Kabir

Aamna... Aamna, Aamna, Aamna…

I had been rolling her name around in my head for days, like a coin on a table, the sound of it familiar by now, but no less painful every time I thought of it. I wanted to be with her so badly, but I knew that I had to give her space. Perhaps she would come back to me by herself? Or maybe she was done with me, my face and this place holding the memories of a rawness that she didn't want to face up to again.

Chhaya had been in touch a few times since our last date, when I had broken things off, but I had chosen to ignore her for the time being. I knew there was something up with her and her family and I didn't want to have to deal with whatever it was right now. I had enough going on already.

Rashi had been very busy of late and I had been avoiding her. She saw something in me when I had told her Aamna had left, and I didn't want to restart that conversation. But if I was being honest with myself, I was worried that I would use Rashi as a way to track her down, to find Aamna and connect with her again, when I knew that what mattered now was giving her the space that she had made it so clear she needed.

I assumed she had returned to her family. That was what had to have happened. But that didn't make it any easier for me to handle her vanishing. I just wanted to see her one more time, to ask her if there was anything that I had done wrong, some mistake I had made that had scared her away. She didn't owe me an explanation, but I knew that I was going to be second-guessing our entire relationship for as long as I lived if I didn't get something in the way of a reason behind her leaving me so abruptly.

And it felt as though things had been going so well, too. That was the hardest part. If I had sensed her drifting away from me, had felt her moving on to a different part of her life, then that would have been different. I could have encouraged her on then, have understood what had driven her away from me. But as it was now, I felt like my life was catching its breath, waiting to continue the next sentence, as though the penny hadn't dropped after her leaving me. I knew I wanted her back, so badly it made my heart ache, so badly it kept me up at night for hours. But I had no idea how I was meant to do that. If I was meant to do it at all…

I was sitting at my desk at work, still thinking about her, knowing that I should have been focusing on the project before me that I was meant to be taking care of. I was giving the go-ahead to a new campaign for a fresh client, and it was important that we got it right to guarantee them coming back for more. But all of this felt so distant and unimportant. And, in that moment, I knew I had to see her – just one last time before I let go – if I had any hope of moving on with my life.

I managed to get through the rest of my day by promising myself that as soon as I got home, I would allow myself to start trying to find her. Not idly, as I had been doing, but truly. I would locate her, make sure she was safe and that she was happy, and then I would be able to move on. Once I had said goodbye and given her everything she needed to build the life that she so sorely deserved to have.

When I arrived back at my apartment, I opened my laptop on the couch and stared at the blank screen for a long time. How was I meant to come across her again? I had to assume that she'd left to her parents' place, so I decided to start there.

Searching her name, I managed to come across an appeal for information that had been released four years before, around the time that she had first gone missing. The picture showed her parents, drawn and pale and exhausted, standing outside what I assumed was their house – a small, humble place, but well-appointed for what it was. I squinted at the picture, downloading it and pulling it up on a program that would allow me to get a closer look, and enhanced the edges and the details until I came across something that would guide me to where I needed to go.

And then I saw it – a street name. Just the corner of a sign, but it was enough. Not far from Lodhi Road. My heart spun in my chest as I realized how close she could have been to me. All this time, it had felt like an endless distance was separating us, but now that distance had narrowed, and she was so close I could almost feel her presence.

I checked the area code of the phone number against the location I believed the house to be and confirmed that I was right in my assumption. I closed my laptop and paced the villa a few times, from top to bottom, trying to work off the excess energy that was forcing me to just get down there already. I should give it some time, leave it till tomorrow, let my brain come to terms with the thought of seeing her again. But I couldn't. It had to be now, it had to be tonight. If I wanted to get a good night's sleep again, I had to see her in person and confirm for myself once and for all that she was alright and happy and safe.

I gathered my things and called my driver, my heart pounding at the notion of seeing her once again. What would I say? I had no idea, but I figured that it would come to me once I was right in front of her once more. The thought of gazing into her eyes again, of being able to spill everything that had been weighing on my shoulders all this time, already felt like a relief. Perhaps it was selfish of me, a chance for me to unload everything I had been carrying all this time on to her. Or perhaps she wanted to see me too. Maybe she missed me the same way I had missed her. I could only hope…

I made my way through the city, the car cutting quietly through the streets as I gazed out into the darkness beyond. The place felt dangerous when it was like this, as though there could have been anything lurking in the shadows beyond. I shivered when I thought of what could be out there – I knew that the terrible place Aamna had been trapped in couldn't be the only one of its kind out there, that my sister was working tirelessly to bring as many of them down as she could. How many other women were trapped in the blackest place in the world, their bodies and minds broken for use by men who were more monsters than they were human?

The car turned on to the street I was sure the house was on, and I leaned forward to speak to the driver directly.

"Slow down," I instructed him. "I'm not sure what I'm looking for, but I know it's here."

I felt a warmth run through me as I looked around – to think, this is where Aamna had grown up. I had been to the neighborhood so many times when I had visited Delhi with my parents, growing up. We had been so close then... Both of us going about our lives, not knowing that the other was so nearby. Who knows what would have happened had the two of us met sooner than we had? No Chhaya, that would have been for sure. Maybe I could have averted her kidnapping.

But I couldn't linger on that. I needed to focus on the here and now, what was right in front of me. My eyes widened as we came across the house that had been in that photograph. I was sure of it, the door the same faded red as it had been when her parents had stood before it to beg for the return of their little girl. I wished I could have been there with her, when she had met them again, when she had walked into the arms of the family who must have been sure they had lost her for good.

"Here?" My driver glanced at me in the mirror, and I hesitated for a moment before replying. This was my last chance to back out, to let her go.

"Here," I finally replied. I had to see her. One more time. To assure myself that she was where she needed to be.

The car drew to a halt, and I stepped out and stood there before the house for a moment before I approached. There was a light on, casting a warm glow out on to the street, so I knew somebody was home. I took deep breaths as I approached the door, pausing for another moment before I knocked. Did I really want to do this? Did I really want to drag her back to that place she had been when she had first arrived at my home, when she had been so vulnerable and so pained and struggling to get through the day?

Before I could overthink it a moment further, I knocked on the door, three hard taps, and waited for someone to respond. I wasn't taking her anywhere or demanding anything from her.

I just needed to know she was safe. At least, that's what I told myself.

I heard movement inside the house, and I shifted my weight from one foot to the other as I waited for someone to answer. If she opened the door, I didn't know what I would do. Throw my arms around her, kiss her, hold her? I glanced over my shoulder and saw my driver watching me curiously; he shifted his gaze from me as soon as he saw me looking at him, and I knew I at least had to play it cool at first, to keep from any gossip spreading amongst the staff.

After a few moments, the woman from the picture opened the door. She looked as though she had aged ten years in the time since the photograph had been taken– her dark hair, wound into a tight bun on the back of her head, was now streaked with grey, and her eyes looked tired, as though she hadn't had a good night's sleep in weeks. I could see hints of Aamna in her, in the shape of her jaw and the curve of her mouth, and I smiled as soon as I laid my eyes on her.

"Hello," I nodded to her politely. "I'm sorry to disturb you at such a late hour. I'm here to see Aamna."

As soon as that name came out of my mouth, her face dropped. I had heard the phrase before, but never seen it acted out with such blatancy – it looked as though her features had slipped from her head, everything sliding downwards when she heard the name of her daughter. After a moment, her head snapped back up, and her eyes met mine, blazing with anger.

"What is this, some kind of joke?" She demanded, her voice cracking. "Aamna hasn't lived here in years."

"What?"

Panic sent my head spinning and my heart pounding out of control.

"What's going on?" A heavy voice called from inside the house, and a moment later the man from the picture wandered out to join his wife. He took one look at the expression on her face, and then turned his attention to me, his eyes burning.

"What are you doing here?" He took a protective step in front of her, and I tried to gather myself in the face of what I had just heard.

"You are Aamna's parents, right?" I planted my hand on the doorframe, hoping it would be enough to keep me upright. My knees felt as though they were going to buckle out from underneath me. The man furrowed his brow at me, his mouth twisting into a mess of pain and anger.

"Yes," he replied finally, after a long pause. "But we don't take any interviews about her anymore. None of them have come to anything, and I don't want any more vultures—"

"I'm not here to interview about her," I told him quickly. "I… I think I need to talk to you."

"You've heard from her?" Her mother's eyes widened, and her face filled with hope, and I instantly felt a rush of guilt knowing that I was going to have to let her down. Yes, I had heard from her, but now she was gone, and I had been the one to let her slip through my fingers. How could I have been so stupid? She would never have left me without letting me know what was happening, where she was going. Something awful had happened to her, and I had no idea what it was or where she might be because of it. My hands were trembling as I pushed them through my hair, trying to calm myself enough to speak.

"She was staying with me," I told them, and her father stepped towards me, pressing his face into mine.

"You're the one who took her?" he snarled, and it was clear that he would have pushed me down the street right now. I shook my head and raised my hands.

"She came to me a few weeks ago," I explained hurriedly, and the woman eyed me for a moment, and then caught her husband's arm and pulled him back.

"Let him in," she ordered him quietly, and, after a moment, he did as he was told. The woman took me by the arm and guided me inside the house, to a small living room where she gestured for me to take a seat down on the couch.

"You know where our daughter is?" she asked, her voice so small and so hopeful that it broke my heart. I shook my head, hating that I had to let them down like this.

"Uma, he doesn't know anything," the man declared as he marched into the room behind us. "We shouldn't even be giving him any time. He's just another one of those vultures who want to profit from our daughter—"

"I'm not, sir, I promise you," I told him urgently. I knew that every moment we spent here was a moment that Aamna was out there, in the world at large, facing the kind of danger that I could only imagine. Where the hell was she?

"I need you to listen to me," I told him quickly. "I know where your daughter's been the last few years, but I don't know where she is now. And I need your help in trying to get her back."

"Tell me about her," Uma, her mother, ordered me. There was still clearly a hint of suspicion in her eyes, and she needed me to prove that I really did know her daughter as well as I claimed to before she gave me a moment of her time or energy.

"Aamna," I took a deep breath and recalled everything that I had learned about that woman who had lived with me for a few weeks. "She wears an anklet on her right foot. She loves to read.

She has – she has these eyes, these incredible eyes, and sometimes they feel like they're going to go straight through you…"

Uma slapped a hand over her mouth and turned to her husband. Her eyes were wide, and even he seemed shaken by what I had just said.

"Manohar," she breathed to him. "It's her. He knows her."

Manohar, her father, stared at me for a long moment, and I saw something crack and break behind his eyes. Perhaps he had been too scared to embrace the possibility of there being some reality to what I was telling him, too nervous to admit that yes, I really might know his daughter. I wondered how long it had been since they had accepted that their daughter was long gone from this place – how long it had been since they had accepted that they would just have to go on without her. And now, here I was, telling them that she was alive – or at least, had been up until a couple of weeks ago.

"Where was she?" Manohar demanded furiously. I knew his anger wasn't directed at me, but it still caught me off-guard.

"She was kidnapped," I told him quickly. "By a… by a pimp."

I didn't want to have to come out and say the words, but I knew I couldn't hide the truth from them forever. Uma closed her eyes and swallowed heavily, as though keeping down the rush of emotion that came with finding out the truth.

"She was kept… they used her, for a few years," I explained hurriedly. "But my sister, she works with this shelter, and they broke everyone out of that place. There wasn't room at the shelter on the first night for Aamna, and she came to stay with me for a while, and we…"

I trailed off, realizing I was facing her parents here and that they may not want to hear about the romantic life of their only daughter.

"I fell in love with her," I continued, the first time I had ever let myself say those words out loud. I was surprised by how good they felt coming out of my mouth, that there was no doubt wrapped up within them, no question in my mind as to whether they were true.

"But a few weeks ago, I woke up and she was gone," I glanced between the two of them. "She'd mentioned her family in the city, and I assumed she'd come down here to stay with the two of you. I came here to check that she was alright and to say goodbye, but…"

"But she's not here," Uma finished up for me. She turned to her husband, her forehead furrowed and her eyes wild with a mix of emotion.

"Manohar, do you hear that?" she demanded of her husband. "Our daughter could be out there. She could be out there…"

"How long has it been since she went missing?" Manohar asked me.

"A couple of weeks," I shook my head. "I'm sorry, I know I should have gone after her sooner, but after everything she'd been through, I didn't want to pressure her—"

"What do we do now?" Manohar demanded. "Where could she be?"

"I have no idea," I confessed. "But I think I might know someone who does."

"Get them over here, now," he ordered me, and I reached for my phone and went to call Rashi. As I left the room, Uma sank in her husband's arms, tears streaming down her face. I couldn't even begin to imagine what she was going through. The daughter she had likely written off as dead long ago was back, but still in danger somewhere far from here. She was so close to having her again, and yet so far. I paced up and down outside the small house as I waited for Rashi to pick up the phone, not caring much about the attention of my driver as he watched me like a hawk.

"Kabir?" Rashi eventually picked up the phone, sleepy. "What's going on? Are you alright?"

"Yeah, I'm fine," I told her. "Could you get down to an address across the city? I'll send the car along to pick you up. I really need you here. It's to do with Aamna."

"Sure, sure," she replied, yawning. "Is everything alright?"

"No idea," I replied truthfully. "But we need you here."

"I'm on my way," she promised me, and I hung up the phone and sent my driver across the city to Rashi's place, so I could get her down here sooner rather than later. I waited outside the house and tilted my head back to the black sky above me – I wanted this to be over, as much as they did. I wanted her back in my arms. And I couldn't believe that I had let her go for so long without chasing her down. I had let myself get distracted by Chhaya, and now Aamna could be in terrible danger – if she was even still alive. No, no. I couldn't let myself think that. I had to focus on the positive, for as long as I could.

Rashi arrived after a significant wait, and she climbed out of the car and gave me a tight hug as soon as she saw me.

"What was that for?" I asked as I pulled back.

"You look as though you need it," she eyed me, stepping back to look me up and down. "Now, are you going to tell me what's going on?"

"Come inside," I jerked my head towards the house. "I have some people I think you should meet."

She followed me in, and Manohar and a tearful Uma leapt to their feet as soon as they saw us approaching.

"Who's this?" Manohar demanded, looking Rashi up and down. "Can she help?"

"This is my sister, Rashi," I explained, as she greeted both of them. "She works at the shelter that saved Aamna in the first place. If anyone can help with this, she can."

"What's going on?" Rashi demanded. "Kabir, who are these people?"

"They are Aamna's parents."

"Then where's Aamna?" she asked, and I shook my head.

"That's what we're trying to find out," I told her. "She vanished from the apartment a couple of weeks ago and I had assumed that she had just come here to live with her parents for a while after everything that had happened. I came here to say goodbye tonight, and then I found that she isn't here at all."

"So, where is she?" Rashi asked again, not getting her head around what I was saying. I shook my head once more.

"We don't know, Rashi," I told her. "But we need your help finding out where she is."

"Oh my god," she rubbed her hand over her face, and Manohar and Uma watched her with withdrawn, nervous faces.

"Alright, well, chances are she's been taken by someone from her old life," Rashi looked up once more, sliding back into professional mode just like that.

"Like who?" Uma asked nervously.

"Like, perhaps an ex-client, or a pimp," Rashi explained, and Uma flinched at the very thought of it. I wanted to tell my sister to show a little restraint, given that she was around the parents of this girl who had been used and abused in such a terrible way, but I knew we didn't have time for politeness.

"Kabir, was there anything she said to you in the last few days before she went, that suggested where her head might have been?" She turned to me. I shook my head.

"But she did say she saw her ex-pimp when we were out together," I replied, drawing my mind back to that time in the mall when she had frozen on the spot and insisted we get out of there at once. I could still recall her sobbing in the back of the car, her entire body wracked with the pain of it, as though she would never truly find a way out from beneath it. My heart twisted. Why hadn't I taken her more seriously then? I had assumed it was her mind playing tricks on her or something, but I should have locked down the villa and set armed security on patrol twenty-four-seven to keep him and anyone else who might have come poking around.

"Shekhar, right?" Rashi raised her eyebrows at me. "That's the name the rest of the girls gave us."

"Yes, I think that's what she said," I nodded. Uma and Manohar were watching the conversation bounce between us, eyes sliding back and forth as though they were watching a tennis match.

"Alright," Rashi nodded, taking a deep, shaky breath like she was trying to cool herself off. "So, we know he was around there. But how could he have gotten to her?"

"I don't know," I shook my head. "The villa is on lockdown every night. Nobody could have gotten in without my say-so, and I was sleeping right next to her, so it wasn't like they could just steal her away from beside me without me noticing." I immediately realized the mistake of my words. Rashi shot me a peculiar look, but didn't say anything. I knew now I would have to explain my relationship with Aamna to her.

"So, she must have gotten out some other way," Rashi spoke after a long pause. She got to her feet and began to pace back and forth. "Kabir, did you notice things missing when you woke up and realized she was gone?"

"Some of the books I'd bought for her," I replied. "Some of the clothes, too. But not everything. She didn't take much."

"See, I don't think a kidnapper would have stood around waiting for her to pick out the books and clothes she likes," she shook her head. "Maybe she left of her own accord. Maybe she really was planning to come down here, and she got intercepted."

"What do you mean?" Uma's eyes were burning with pain upon hearing that her daughter really could have been searching for them. As I glanced around the room, I noticed how dissonant the expensive furniture and accoutrements seemed in a place like this, and then it struck me – they must have stayed in this house all this time, despite the fact that they could afford something nicer, in case Aamna ever came home. My heart broke for them, and I swore at that moment that I would find a way to reunite Aamna with her family.

"Kabir, did anything happen that night? Anything at all?" Rashi demanded of me, and I blinked and tried to push my mind back. I had been so shaken-up that day that I hadn't really taken in much at all, so devastated that Aamna had left me. But then I remembered – the text from Chhaya.

"I got a message from Chhaya that night," I blurted out. "Aamna could have seen it. Maybe she thought I was cheating on her?"

"That could have been the push she needed to get out of there," Rashi screwed her eyes and nodded. "But not without grabbing a few bits and pieces before she left. And if Shekhar had seen her recently, he might have stalked her back to the house, and when she was out in the middle of the night all by herself..."

She trailed off, but she didn't need to fill in the rest. I stared at her for a long moment.

"You're saying that her ex-pimp has her?" I demanded, and she nodded.

"I think it's our best bet," she replied. "If she saw him around shortly before she went missing, then we must assume that he saw her too. And that he's doing everything he can right now to get some of the control he lost back. She could just be a side effect of that."

"Oh my god!" I buried my head in my hands, and Manohar reached over to take Uma's hand and squeezed it tightly. I forced myself to look up. These people needed me. Aamna needed me. I couldn't sit around being upset when there was so much work that needed to be done.

"What now?" I asked Rashi, who was already on her feet.

"Kabir, give me your phone," she held her hand out. "Can I use your driver, too?"

"Anything you need," I assured her, and she squeezed my shoulder.

"Can I talk to you outside?" she spoke pointedly, and I knew it was time to reveal the truth of my relationship.

The moment we were alone outside, she smacked me on my shoulder, "What the hell Kabir?" she hissed angrily. "I left Aamna in your care so that she could be protected, not that you start sleeping in her bed and…" she trailed off. I couldn't believe what she was insinuating.

"Are you insane? I was not using or abusing her," I exclaimed pulling my hair. "Yes, we were in a relationship," I started to explain, but the wild look in Rashi's eyes stopped me.

"Relationship with *her?* You think mom-dad would accept it?" she demanded. I didn't know if she was worried or angry.

"I don't care about them as of now. All I care is that I love her, and I want her back and safe next to me," I yelled.

"You love her?" Rashi couldn't believe me.

"Can we get on this topic later? Can you please focus your energy on finding her, instead of wondering what may or may not happen in my love life?" I demanded agitated. Every second here was crucial, and I felt this conversation was futile.

She gave me a long searching look and then marched inside.

"What's going on?" Manohar demanded, clearly agitated with the wait. Uma was clinging hopelessly on his arm, and I could see how broken they must be feeling.

"We'll find her, Kabir," Rashi spoke after a while and promised me. Then she turned to Manohar and Uma. "And we'll bring your daughter home."

Uma closed her eyes, and a single tear ran down her cheek. I stared at the empty seat beside them, and I could almost see Aamna in it – laughing, her legs tucked up beneath her, a book sitting on the arm of the chair with the page folded down, so she could come back to it later. I was going to make that a reality, no matter what. I was going to make sure that Aamna was safe again.

14

Aamna

I looked at myself in the tainted bathroom mirror. Under my eyes, bags that had faded to purple told me that I wasn't getting enough rest – my lips were cracked and dry, and my skin was dusty and needed care. My hair, scraped back into a bun to keep it out of my way, was a mess. And yet, there was something in my eyes that I hadn't seen in a long time. Resolve.

I drew myself up to my full height and smiled at myself in the mirror. It had been so long since I had smiled that I felt as though I was faking it, the muscles of my face tugging awkwardly to get it to stick. But I didn't have to convince myself. I just had to convince Shekhar, for long enough to get him out of here. And then I was going to make a break for it.

I had been here for almost a month. I had kept track of the days, hoping that the knowledge would keep me from going utterly out of my mind. Sometimes, it felt as though I was going to burst, my brain aching with the pain of knowing there was a whole life for me out there, a whole life that he insisted on keeping from me until I gave in to what he seemed to want from me.

Ever since the day I had dared speak back to him, that day he had sent pots and pans crashing around the kitchen to express his fury, things had only gotten worse. He hadn't laid a finger on me – I had warned him, told him that men who loved women did not harm them, and he seemed to have taken it to heart, thank god! But he had taken to damaging anything else in the apartment that he could get his hands on to scare me into submission. He had tipped the bed over, sent the mattress flying from the metal frame; he had slammed his fist into the hand mirror in the bathroom, sending shattered glass everywhere, including into his own knuckles. He had kicked a hole in the wall next to the door. With every day that passed, I knew my safety was growing less and less certain, that it would only be a matter of time before he snapped and turned his anger on me. And I had to use what little time I had to my advantage.

I was running out of time. I knew that he could only keep up the façade of himself being a decent man for a little longer before he broke and forced me to submit to his will. Hell, before I was rescued, I would already had given in, let him do what he wanted to me just to get it over with. He had trained me hard enough when I had worked for him to do as I was told with no exceptions, and certainly, no questions. But I had stepped out of his world, seen what was beyond it, that there was love and care and passion that grew organically instead of being exchanged for money per hour. And I wasn't going to walk away from that. Not yet.

My resolve grew strong as I lay in bed after one of his more violent outbursts, trying to avoid the spot in the bed frame where he had arched the metal such that it jabbed into my back as I tried to sleep. I had to get out of here. I had to try at least.

He rarely left the place, and whenever he did, he always came back very soon. Also, every time he went away, he would make sure to lock the doors tight behind him, so I had no hope of getting out. But his absence at least gave me the time I needed to check out the rest of the place. There were three windows – one in the living room, a tiny one in the bathroom, and one in the bedroom that he slept in, that led out onto a tiny balcony beyond.

We were high up in the building, so I could hardly leap down from there and onto the street. But recently I had spotted a small fire escape, one that looked as though it was on the brink of falling apart, a half-dozen feet from the balcony – it would be quite a jump, but I could make it if I tried. If I had the time to try. The window that led out onto the balcony was locked shut, where the rest of them were sealed tight with glue. It explained why the air felt like it was suffocating me in here, why sometimes I felt as though I was going to drown under the weight of it.

The lock was slim and flimsy, I knew that much. I headed out of the bathroom, where I had been noting the resolve in my eyes and promising myself that I was going to double my efforts and slipped into his bedroom. He was out for some food, and I didn't know how long I had before he made it back. This time he had taken much longer than usual. I tried to break the lock with my hands, but came out with nothing but welts on my palms for my efforts. I would need to find something stronger to snap it. I had no idea what I might use, and before I had a chance to look, Shekhar burst back into the house.

"Aamna?" he called and I dived from his room to mine, knowing that if he found me in here, he would take it as the come-on he was looking for. The thought of his hands on me made my stomach turn. To feel him touch me like that again, as though he owned some piece of my body and my soul, would end me. I couldn't let him do that. I couldn't let him do anything.

"In here!" I called back, trying to keep my voice bright. I knew that I needed to start convincing him that I was coming around to his twisted little game. That was the only chance I had of getting out. He loved me, or so he claimed, but he didn't trust me. And I had to find a way to build that trust, that sureness.

"Were you in my room?" he demanded, eyeing me suspiciously. I shook my head.

"Of course not," I replied, my voice sounding saccharine-sweet to my ears, but he smiled.

"I missed you while I was away," he said and sat down on the edge of the bed. When he took my hand, I let him, even though I wanted nothing more than to whip it away from him and tell him off for daring to lay a hand on me. He stared down at our fingers, connected, and it appeared as he was waiting for me to pull back. I didn't.

"Aamna," he began again, and I fought the urge to roll my eyes. I could tell another one of his speeches was coming. He kept on giving me these long-winded declarations of his love, of the ways he had changed, of the life he would give me. I knew they had more to do with him than they did with me. He just saw me as a conduit to prove what a good person he was, although he had done some of the most evil things I had ever known a human to do in my life.

"Aamna, I know that things have been hard with us," he told me, opening my palm and tracing his fingers over it in a gesture that he no doubt believed was the height of romance. I winced, glad that he was looking away because I couldn't keep the disgust at his touch off my face.

"But I know that we can build a beautiful life together," he continued. "I know that you can change me. You already have. I've never felt this way about someone before…"

I fought the urge to scream at him, to tell him that it wasn't my job to fucking change him, that he shouldn't rely on me to make him a good person, and that nothing he could do would pick apart the monstrousness of what he had already done to me. That he had broken me and that I wouldn't let him put me back together. But I didn't. The best I could do was stay silent and nod, hoping that my disdain for him wasn't coming off me in waves.

"I love you, baby," he murmured to me, and he leaned over to kiss me. I twisted my face at the last moment so he got my cheek, unable to yet handle his kiss on the mouth. The last person I had kissed was Kabir, and I felt as though I was preserving that kiss on my lips, the memory of it, and the joy of his embrace.

"Mmm…" I let out a little noise that I hoped could pass off for agreement. He smiled and got to his feet.

"Come with me," he ordered. "I brought some food from a very fancy restaurant. It was quite far away, but I thought it would cheer you up. You can set it down for me."

I looked up at him; still not able to understand that he really believed this was romance. I almost felt sorry for him. What kind of fucked-up world had he been raised in that he truly believed getting me to do chores for him was the height of some romantic seduction? He looked down at me, clear-eyed and sure, and I smiled back. The muscles felt like they were straining once more, but I didn't care. He seemed to believe anything that I gave him in the hopes that it meant I was finally giving in to him, and I wasn't going to argue with his interpretation.

I rose to my feet and followed him into the dingy kitchen – most of the pots and pans were bruised and dented from where he had used them to express his fury at some point over the last few weeks, but I pretended not to notice that and looked at the food he had brought with him.

I had never much learned how to cook; my mother had often suggested teaching me, but I had always assumed it was the kind of skill I would pick up somewhere down the line, once I was living by myself and had no choice but to learn how to cook. I felt a twist in my stomach as I thought about everything this man had taken from me, and suddenly, just like that, I had met my edge.

I would never have a normal life, not after what I had been through. And he had been the one to rip that from me, the one who would keep taking that from me, unless I took a stand right here and now. Every moment that I spent here with him, every second I let myself sink further into this life he was trying to make for us, it was another moment I couldn't go out into the world and be the person I wanted to be, the person he had tried to keep from me. It wasn't just Kabir he had stolen me from, it was myself, the woman that I knew was aching for a release. And that woman wasn't going to put up with this a second longer.

I closed the bags and turned back to him. My heart was pounding, and I could feel the fearful panic rising in my throat, but I had to do it. He was sitting at the dining room table, looking up at me expectantly, his hands resting on his thighs. He was clenching them both, as though he was trying to contain something. And I knew he had to think of himself as a great and noble man for not grabbing me right there and then and forcing me to do what he wanted.

I sank into the seat next to him and looked him in the eyes, the eyes of the man who had stolen my entire life from me. Well, he wasn't going to get away with it. Not a chance.

"Shekhar," I began, and even his name felt filthy in my mouth. As soon as this was over, I wasn't going to say his name ever again. I was going to banish him from my mind, and he was going to rot without me.

"I know I have been difficult," I shook my head, lowering my gaze in what I hoped he would read as deference to him. "And I know that I have made it hard for you..."

"You have," he agreed at once, a spiked edge to his voice, as though he intended to hurt me.

"But I think I see now," I continued, ignoring his interruption. "I think I understand what you want from me."

"You do?" he perked up at once, his eyes brightening. He grabbed my hand, and I let it lay limply against his.

"I want to be with you," I told him, forcing the words out even though they felt dirty on my lips. "But I need you to make a promise to me."

"Anything," he assured me at once, and there was a triumphant look on his face, as though he couldn't believe this was really happening. How stupid was he, to believe that I would just give in to him like this? Did he really see this as atonement for what he had done to me for so long? I would never forgive him as long as I lived. But I just had to get through this, and then it would be over. For good.

"You've been with so many women," I continued. "I want you to show that you're committed to me."

"I'll do anything," he replied, tracing his eyes up and down my body in a way that made me feel ill. How many times had he taken me without my consent? How many times had he given me that look before he had done it?

"Anything?" I raised my eyebrows at him.

"Anything," he repeated, his voice full of certainty and something I could have mistaken for sincerity if I hadn't been looking too closely.

"I want a ring," I told him, looking deep into his eyes, trying to connect with the man beneath this monster. I felt a little twist of guilt – even though I hated him, he seemed to really want me, and I never liked having to indulge in this kind of manipulation, even if he was totally deserving of it.

"A ring?" His eyes lit up, as though he had been expecting me to ask for something much worse than that. "What kind?"

"I don't care," I replied, a nip of impatience in my voice that I swiftly worked to quell. "I mean… anything you want. I trust you to pick out something perfect for me."

He smiled at me, and before I could stop him, he leaned forward and planted a kiss on my lips. Everything in me shuddered at the horror of his touch, and I forced myself not to pull back and shove him away. My mouth was hard and unyielding, but I was still letting him do this, letting him convince himself that the two of us were really a thing now.

He leaned back and eyed me for a moment, and there was an air of triumph to him, as though he had finally won at a game he had been playing for months.

"I knew you'd come around to me, love," he reached out to stroke my face, and I felt my entire body seize up at his touch. I forced myself to endure it, promising my mind that I would be out of here soon enough.

"I just need to see that you really mean the things you say," I replied, my voice sounding distant and removed, as though it was coming from someone else entirely. I hated the way the words sounded coming out of my mouth, but I had to do this. I had to get him out of here.

"I do," he widened his eyes at me. "I do, Aamna."

"I need that ring," I repeated myself firmly, "Before I can trust you."

He sighed deeply, and a flash of irritation passed across his face. For a moment, I was sure he was going to lash out at me, finally tired of my attempts to get him to do what I wanted. But then he softened again and shook his head.

"I'll expect a reward for my efforts," he replied, his eyes trailing over my body suggestively. "I've missed having you so much, Aamna..."

"As soon as you're back," I promised him. "But I need to know you mean this."

"Fine," he got to his feet and went to collect his things. A rush of relief passed through me as I watched him preparing to leave, mixed with a panic that I was doing my best to keep down. If I couldn't get out of here while he was away, he would expect me to give myself to him once more. And the thought of his hands on my body, erasing and wiping clean the memory of Kabir, made my heart ache.

He planted one more kiss on my cheek before he left, and I sat there for a moment at the table, listening to his footsteps as they retreated down the stairs until they faded into nothingness. I got to my feet swiftly, testing the door to see if he might have left it unlocked by some miracle of chance, but it was firmly shut. I grimaced. So I had to go out of that window.

I scrabbled through the cutlery drawer, grabbing whatever I could that looked as though it might have enough tensile strength to pop the cheap metal lock off the window. I found a couple of things – a wooden spoon, a knife, a spatula – and I headed through to the bedroom, armed with my findings, and went to make my escape attempt.

My heart was racing, and my hands were shaking as I slid the wooden spoon under the loop of the lock and pried it backwards. If Shekhar walked in on me doing this, there would be no denying what my actual plan had been and I would pay for my attempt to get out of here. He would know I had been lying to him, and then what? How would he burn me for my mistruths? Would he see me as useless, now that he knew he couldn't trust me? And what did useless mean to a man like him? I knew what became of the girls he had run out of purpose for, and it was far from pretty.

I forced myself to push those eventualities out of my mind and pushed harder on the wooden spoon. I heard a click, and the loop of the lock popped up by a half-centimeter. My heart leapt, and I pulled the spook away and tried to pry the lock apart with my hands, but I couldn't get a grip under the metal. I let out a frustrated groan and reached for one of the smaller knives I'd brought through, trying to press it into the tiny space between the loop that was holding the lock closed and the brassy metal of the lock itself.

It slipped out a couple of times, mostly thanks to my trembling fingers, but finally, it found purchase and I was able to pry the lock a little further open. I tossed the knife aside and went to work with the spoon once more, pressing the end to the windowsill to create more leverage. Suddenly, with a loud metal clang, the lock popped off, landing on the floor below me. My heart leapt. *I had done it.* But it was far from over yet.

The window had been shut for god knows how long, and it seemed as though it had all but sealed itself together as I went to push it open again. I had to slide two of the knives below the window to pry it open a crack, and then press down on them both at once, using what little strength I had left in my body to push it open. An inch of daylight, real air, streamed in, and I gasped with relief. My scrabbling fingers pushed it open further, all the while my ears pricked to the sound of Shekhar coming back and catching me in the act. Elation, fear, dread, relief – I couldn't keep my head straight. But I didn't have to. I just had to get out of here.

I forced the window open and grabbed one of the knives from the windowsill, tucking it into my trousers as I slipped out of the small space I had created. My foot got caught, the window sliding down suddenly and catching me off-guard, but I managed to wrench it free and drag myself out onto the tiny balcony below. It wobbled dangerously, and I knew it wouldn't hold out long, so I scrambled to the fire escape I had seen next to it.

As soon as I had tossed my leg over the edge of the balcony and on to the flimsy metal steps, I felt it shudder under my weight. This thing probably hadn't been used in years, and for good reason. I swallowed back my fear and started to climb down, going slow, reminding myself that I was out of there now and that he wouldn't be able to just drag me back in again without a fight. I wrapped my fingers around the knife in my pocket to confirm its presence. There was no way I was letting him pull me back there. I would cut off his hands, those hands that had touched me, before I let him do that.

I made my way down the steps as fast as I could, without them giving out entirely from beneath me, and I looked down at the street below, wondering where the hell I was. That would be another thing; I would have to find some way back to somebody who could keep me safe. What was to say that I wouldn't run into another bastard down on the street? The world apparently is filled with them! *Focus, focus...* I could think about that once I was actually down there. For the time being, the only thing that mattered was getting off these steps, and as far from the apartment as I possibly could.

I finally rounded the last set of what had seemed like endless stairs, and I dropped with a thud onto the pavement below. My heart was pounding so hard that I was sure it would burst out of my chest, and I glanced around fearfully, certain that I could sense Shekhar somewhere nearby. Maybe this had all been a test for me, and now that I had failed it, he would see no need to hold back on his cruelty.

And, as I flicked my eyes around the street, I saw him. And everything came to a grinding halt.

15

Kabir

"Are you sure we're in the right place?" I asked Rashi, fidgeting next to her in the car. She reached over and patted my shoulder.

"I'm sure we are," she assured me. "It's going to be alright, Kabir. We're going to get her safe again." Rashi had turned the world upside down to find Aamna ever since I had declared my love for her, and I owed big time to her.

I turned to look out of the window and tried to take her words to heart, but it was hard when all I wanted was to see the woman I loved safe once more.

And we had worked so hard to get to this point. I chewed my lip as we drew up on to the street where he was meant to be staying, and forced myself to take a deep breath. This was going to be fine. I had to keep telling myself that. Then I actually might start to believe it.

In the car behind us, Aamna's parents were following close behind. If this was hard for me, I couldn't imagine how hard it had been for them; to think that their daughter, the one they had been so sure was lost forever, had been so close and yet so far to them. And that even now she could be in a danger that they wouldn't be able to save her from.

I had worked closely with them ever since we had put the pieces together and realized where she had been taken, and while they had done their best to keep their game faces on, I could tell that the agony of this was burning them from the inside, the same way it was burning me.

"What do we do?" Uma had asked helplessly, as Rashi and I paced around their living room, trying to figure out the best way to approach this mess.

"We need to start by running down everything that we know about her," Rashi kneeled next to Uma, and took her hand. I felt a swell of pride seeing her like that. My sister had such a deep well of compassion within her, and I knew that I wouldn't have been able to get through any of this if it hadn't been for her.

"And how do we do that?" I asked her. She turned to me.

"I'll talk to all the girls we have down in the shelter right now," she informed. "And then we take it to the police. They were part of the investigation into the brothel in the first place; they should have some decent information about the people who frequented it and the people who ran it."

I nodded, trying to keep my face from showing the panic I was feeling at that moment. Because I had a feeling I knew exactly who had taken her. That pimp, the one who she had been so certain she had seen at the shopping center. If only I had taken her more seriously then.

Everything kicked into high gear in the days following the revelation – I went with Rashi to the shelter to help out as much as I could. I found myself even more intent on getting Aamna back once I had spent some time with other women who were part of the same brothel. All of them had been hurt in ways I could never imagine. I couldn't believe a human being inflicting such misery on another, and Aamna could be stuck in the middle of that even as I sat there with them.

I lay in bed at night, my arms craving for her. It was something I had never felt before, a true craving for another human being, and I knew it was not physical. I needed her near me because I wanted her safe, and I knew the only way to guarantee that was if we got her out of whatever situation she was trapped in at that moment.

Chhaya had been reaching out to me constantly over the last few days, and I had been doing everything I could to ignore her increasing attention. I just wanted her to go away, to leave me alone, and to give me some space so that I could figure out what we were going to do about Aamna. Any other time, I might have been kinder to her, happier to turn her down more gently than I might have before, but now every time my phone buzzed with a message, and I saw it was from her, I found myself filling with anger. I wanted her gone from my life, but she obviously didn't feel the same way.

After a few days of interviewing the women at the shelter, Rashi moved on to the police. The two of us visited the station together to share the information we had gathered, and to cross-reference it with the stuff they already knew.

"So, you said you were out at a local shopping center when she claimed to have seen her ex-pimp?" The officer, a woman with sharp brown eyes, looked over the paper she was holding at me. I nodded.

"I thought it might just have been a panic attack," I explained. "But I took her home anyway. She was really shaken up by it."

"Did you see him?" she asked me, and she pulled a small black and white photograph out from the file she was holding and pushed it towards me. "Does this ring any bells?"

I looked down at the picture, praying that I would find myself looking at something, anything, we could catch on to and run with, but the man in the photograph didn't seem familiar to me at all. I shook my head and grimaced.

"I don't recognize him," I admitted, and the officer pressed her lips together and frowned.

"I do," Rashi grabbed the photograph. "Shit, I knew I'd seen him somewhere before. He was hanging out near the shelter about a month ago. I thought he was acting shifty, but I didn't put it down to anything. Do you think he was scouting the place out to try and find out where she was?"

"There's a good chance," the officer nodded.

"So where do we find him?" I demanded. "Where could he be?"

"Well, he's only ever operated inside the city," the officer explained. "We've never been able to pin him down to anything, but with the brothel and the testimony of the girls in the shelter, he must know that we're looking for him. Chances are he's trying to lay low somewhere instead of skipping town, so he doesn't attract any attention."

I rubbed my hand over my face. Well, that was something. Maybe Aamna was closer than we thought.

Uma and Manohar wanted to put up 'missing' posters with her face on them all around the city, but we advised against it. It would have tipped Shekhar off that we were looking for him, and the last thing we wanted was for him to make a run for it with Aamna.

"But don't you think it would be better to have her face out there?" Manohar asked. He looked as though he hadn't slept in days.

"We don't even know if he's letting her out of the apartment," Rashi pointed out patiently. "But chances are he's roaming around town right now, and if he sees one of those, he'll make a break for it with your daughter."

"When I get my hands on him, I'm going to..." Manohar trailed off and shook his head, his face tight. Uma squeezed his hand.

"We're going to have our daughter back," she reminded him. "And nothing else is going to matter."

The hunt was on for Shekhar at that point, knowing that he was the one who had taken her. I rolled his name around in my head over and over; testing it out, filling it with such vitriol it seemed to spark like a flame every time it passed through my mind. I was going to ruin him as soon as I got my hands on him. He had no idea what was coming for him.

The cops spread his face and name through the city and alerted all the stations to be on the lookout for him. Later that same day, one of them contacted us with some new information.

"Really?" Rashi gasped down the phone. "That's amazing. We'll be right down. Just give me a minute..."

She hung up and went to grab her stuff. She had been staying at the villa with me for the last few days, her clothes scattered around the place.

"What's going on?" I asked, jumping up from the couch.

"They've got someone who used to work for Shekhar in custody over on the other side of the city," she explained to me. "They say he's willing to talk, and that he might have an idea as to where this guy actually is."

"Thank fuck," I muttered and hurried to get myself ready. Every step we took was a step closer to finding Aamna, even though it felt as though this was all going with a painful slowness. I had to keep myself together, no matter what, and focus on getting her to safety.

We didn't get to sit in on the interview, but the officer working the case with us did, and she came out when it was done with a grin on her face.

"Did you get anything?" Rashi leapt to her feet. The officer nodded and handed us a piece of paper.

"This is a list of the addresses he usually uses," she explained, as I scanned down the paper and took in the half-dozen places on it. "We're going to check all of them out and figure out which one he's actually staying in."

"And then…?" I wondered aloud.

"And we have every reason to think that we're going to find him there," she told me calmly. It was the first time I had seen her smile, and I felt a flood of relief knowing that she seemed to think this case was taking a turn for the better.

They staked out his addresses for the next couple of days, watching for comings and goings, and Rashi and I helped out by bringing sustenance to the officers on the case. Manohar and Uma were at home, texting me every ten minutes for updates. I had gifted them a couple of mobile phones from the company to make sure they could speak to me whenever they wanted, and they were firmly taking advantage of that.

And then, finally, on the third day of stakeouts, I got a call. Exhausted, I lifted myself from the bath I had just climbed into and picked up the phone.

"Hello?"

"Kabir?" It was Uma, her voice cracking with excitement. "They've found him."

"What? Where?"

"One of the apartments, they saw him in the neighboring area. They had never seen him leave the apartment before, so they assume he is using some stealthy entrance and exit all the time. It is the first time he had moved out in the open," she explained, the words flooding out of her as though she had no control over them. "They're sending some people over there now to get in and see if Aamna's there. We're going over. I thought you and your sister would want to come as well."

"Give me the address, and I'll be right over," I agreed, blood pounding in my veins as I took note of the apartment building we had to be at. I got dressed quickly, my hands shaking as I pulled on my clothes. I was so close to her. I could feel it. It was happening.

I came out of the bathroom and found Rashi passed out asleep on the couch. I shook her awake at once, and she blearily opened her eyes and looked up at me with irritation.

"What is it?"

"They found him," I told her, and she snapped upright at once, eyes wide.

"Where?"

"This address," I thrust it into her hand. "They're sending people down there now. We have to go."

"I'm coming, I'm coming," she assured me, grabbing for her shoes and her coat and pulling them on. I was pacing up and down the room, the thoughts in my head going so fast that they were beginning to blur together. If this turned out to be another dead end, I wasn't sure I would be able to take it. I needed to believe that I was about to see her again, that I was mere minutes from holding her in my arms once more.

We sped across the city, and I swear I didn't hear a noise as I made my way through the streets. My mind was in tunnel-vision mode, the only thing I could think about was the woman who needed me. Rashi was beside me, fingers clutching the wheel so tightly that the knuckles looked as though they were going to pop through her fingers. The tension pulsed in the air between us, that unspoken hope that we were going to do this, that it was going to be over in a matter of minutes.

She drew the car to a sharp halt when we arrived at the address, and I spotted Manohar and Uma lingering beside a small cluster of discreet police vehicles tucked down another street.

"What's happening?" I ran over towards them.

"He came back and went out again not long afterwards," Manohar explained, his arm wrapped tight around his wife's shoulders; she was leaning in against him, pressing her head into his shoulder, her chest rising and falling swiftly.

"What are they going to do?" Rashi asked, catching up with me, a little out of breath.

"They said they're going to try and get into the apartment building by force," Manohar glanced over his shoulder towards the spot where the cops were conversing urgently.

"Why are they waiting?" I demanded, raking my hands through my hair. "Why don't they just go up there now?"

"They want to make sure he's far enough away first," Manohar explained. "And give them time to try and put the place back together if she's not there and they need to go back undercover on this thing…"

"They can't wait that long." I shook my head. A certainty was pulsing in my mind, a knowledge that Aamna was nearby. "She's here. I can feel it."

"Kabir, please," Rashi caught my arm, sensing what I was going to do. "You need to give them time; they know what they're doing—"

"I can't risk it." I shook my head. I knew I was acting crazy, but I had to know. I had to see her.

I broke away from the group and turned back towards the apartment building. Rashi immediately gave chase, but I was faster than her. I sped across the street, ignoring the frustrated horns of the cars I sprinted past, and arrived on the sidewalk, looking around desperately. I could feel her. She was so close.

And that's when I saw her.

She landed on the pavement below her with a small thud, leaping from the fire escape that ended a few feet above the ground. She was barefoot, her clothes hanging off her as though she hadn't eaten in days. Her body was trembling as she tried to keep her balance, her eyes wide as she looked around and took in the world around her as though she was laying eyes on it for the first time. And that's when she saw me.

"Kabir!" she cried out, and suddenly I felt my legs powering me towards her. For a moment, I had been sure she was a mirage, some creation of my addled brain that sprang from just wanting to see her so badly. But she wasn't. She was right here in front of me. Everything I needed, everything I wanted, everything I had worked so hard to find.

I caught her before she collapsed to the ground. She was nearly weightless in my arms, and she wound her arms around my neck and held on tight as her legs buckled beneath her.

"Aamna," I murmured in her ear, pulling her in close. I inhaled the scent of her once more, her body fitting against mine like it had been a missing piece all this time. She was shaking so badly it felt as though she might fall away from me once more, like a leaf slipping off a tree, but she sank her fingers into me as though she never intended to let go again.

"We need to get out of here," she pulled back and looked at me, wild-eyed with fear. "Shekhar, he's coming back, and if he finds you—"

"It's okay," I assured her, stroking her hair back from her face. "The police are here. They're going to take care of him. You don't need to worry about it."

"The police are here?" She craned over my shoulder, and I turned to see the whole crew I'd left behind making their way across the road to join me.

"And Rashi," I told her. "And… and your parents."

I swear to god she seemed to stop breathing for a moment when those words came out of my mouth.

"My parents are here?" she asked, her voice tiny. I nodded.

"I thought you'd gone to stay with them, so I tracked them down after you went," I explained. "They've been helping me find you."

"Oh my god," she gasped, and I saw her eyes begin to fill with tears as she looked beyond me once more. Uma and Manohar were hurtling towards us, down the alleyway where she had landed. They crashed into us, the four of us becoming tangled together for a moment as they held their daughter for the first time in years. A few people walking down the street were craning their necks to see what was happening, what all the fuss was about, but I didn't mind their voyeurism. I wanted as many people as possible to see what was happening. It just made it feel all the more real to me.

Uma pulled back, and I slipped my arm around Aamna's waist to keep her upright as her mother grasped her face and looked deep into her eyes.

"I can't believe it's you," she kept saying, over and over. Manohar just seemed gobsmacked, unable to say a word.

"It's me, mama," Aamna replied, a shaky smile spreading over her face. "It's really me."

"My little girl..." Uma hugged Aamna tight once more, pulling her so close that I was afraid Aamna might break.

"Excuse me, ma'am," one of the cops approached. "We need to run a medical examination on you, when you have a moment."

"Go, go," Uma waved her hand, indicating that her daughter should get checked out. "You need it. Go on."

Aamna took my hand, and I followed her over to the cops. She looked so nervous, as though she thought this was all some sick joke and it was going to get torn away from her at any second. I wanted to hold her, to tell her that it was alright and that I would never let anything bad happen to her ever again, but everyone was clustering in around her to make sure she was alright, and I didn't want to overwhelm her. I finally felt a smile spread out across my face as I watched the cops and the medical staff give her a once-over. Rashi stepped to join me, squeezing my shoulder.

"Well, we did it," she told me, and I beamed at her.

"I would never have been able to do it without you," I told her, "Any of it."

"You're the one who brought the family back together," she reminded me, as Manohar and Uma went to fuss over their daughter once more. "You should be proud of yourself."

"I don't think I'm there quite yet," I shook my head. "Not until I know she's safe and healthy."

"She looks okay," Rashi remarked. "Physically, at least. Mentally, it might take a bit of time."

"I don't care," I replied, looking over at Aamna. I had always known being with her might be hard, maybe even harder now, but I would have stuck it out through anything. I knew that now. Nothing had ever been clearer to me in my life.

"You should go be with her," Rashi told me gently. "Don't let her get away. I can tell from the way she looks at you she wants you close to her."

I headed over to join Aamna, as the medical team prodded and poked at her, and she pulled me down next to her, on to the edge of the back of the van she was perched on.

"I can't believe you're really here," she told me again, her voice low as she traced the shape of my face with her fingers. She leaned forward and planted a soft kiss against my lips, and I felt a surge of desire rush through me.

"Miss, please," one of the medical examiners remarked patiently. "We need you to keep as still as possible."

"Sorry, sorry," she waved her hand and smiled, and then turned to her parents. "Besides, I shouldn't be making out in front of my mum and dad, should I?"

"I don't care what you do," Manohar told her. He was still hanging back a little, as though he didn't quite believe this was real and didn't want to get hurt when the truth of it was all revealed, but Uma was kneeling on the ground before her daughter, gazing up at her as though she had risen from the dead. I supposed, to them, it was like she had.

"As long as you're here with us," Uma finished up, and Aamna reached out to squeeze her mother's hands.

"It was a strange way to meet your boyfriend, though," Manohar pointed out with a chuckle, and Aamna and I exchanged looks. *Boyfriend.* We had never used that word to describe our relationship before, and I had no idea what kind of place we were in right now. But she smiled and nodded, then turned back to her father.

"Well, at least I don't have to worry about you disapproving of him, right?" she chuckled. "He saved my life. You have to like him."

"We do," Uma agreed at once, beaming at me. "He's a part of the family now."

"Yeah, he is," Aamna nodded, shooting a look at me and smiling so wide it looked as though her face was going to split in two.

Suddenly, there was a flurry of activity from behind us, and we turned to crane around and see what was happening. Aamna curled her body into mine when she saw Shekhar approaching, but before he could get near her, the cops grabbed him.

"What's going on?" Shekhar demanded, his voice whining and irritating. I wrapped my arm around Aamna and held her close, partly to comfort her and partly to keep from getting to my feet and beating the ever-living shit out of that man.

"You're under arrest," one of the cops told him firmly.

"What the fuck are you—"

Before I could make out anything else, his voice was cut off by the slam of a car door, and I felt a wave of relief pass over me. It was done. We were done with him. He was going to be in jail for a long time, and he couldn't get anywhere near Aamna.

"I want to go home," Aamna raised her gaze to look at me, her eyes burning with sincerity.

"Where?" I asked gently. "To your parents, or…?"

"To your place," she replied, and I glanced at Uma and Manohar. They both nodded.

"Take her where she wants to go," Uma agreed. "We'll be across to visit soon. Maybe Aamna can come home to see us, huh?"

"I would love that," Aamna smiled at her mother, letting her eyes linger on her as though she was trying to commit her to memory.

"But you need your rest now, love," Manohar took his daughter's hand. "We can figure everything out tomorrow, when you're feeling better."

"Thank you," Aamna murmured, and she got to her feet. My arm wrapped tightly around her, and I did the same thing.

"I'll see you soon," Aamna told her parents and then turned to Rashi. "And you, too… Thank you for everything."

"Thank you for leading us to one of the biggest assholes in the city," Rashi replied, and Aamna managed a laugh, though I could tell it was a little strained.

"As long as you don't make me do it again," she warned, and she turned and nestled her head into my shoulder.

I led her to the car and opened the door for her. She climbed in, and sank her head against the seat, letting out a long sigh, as though she was letting all the demons that had filled her up these last few weeks fly free of her. And I watched her, the woman I loved, the woman I finally had back, and I couldn't help but smile. This was exactly how it was meant to be. Her, close to me again, safe in my arms, her family waiting and ready for her when she was. But for now, she wanted it to be just us, and I was more than happy to indulge that for her.

16

Aamna

When we arrived outside the villa, that was when it really sunk in. I felt tears fill my eyes and put my hand over my mouth as it clicked to me that I was really out of the nightmare which I had been caught up in, that bad dream that felt as though it had gone on for a lifetime.

"Are you alright?" Kabir reached across to take my hand, and I nodded.

"I'm just…" I tried to find some way to put my emotions into words, but I came up blank. There wasn't the vocabulary in any language to describe my feelings to him, so I would just have to settle on tears for now. I knew they were happy tears, tears of relief, tears of joy that I had seen my parents again and knew they hadn't rejected me for what I had been through.

"Here," he unbuckled my seatbelt and lifted me into his arms. "Let's get you up to bed, alright?"

I wrapped my arms around him and let him carry me and to the bedroom I had left all those weeks ago. I had truly believed that I would never see this place again, that my punishment for leaving in the night would be a lifetime trapped in that awful apartment with Shekhar, but here I was. And it was far from a fantasy. This was the real world; the man carrying me was a real man. The only real man I had ever truly known.

He lay me down gently in bed, and I let my head sink back into the pillow and closed my eyes. But instead of feeling tired, I felt a sudden rush of energy, my entire body suddenly feeling as though it was sparking with overblown electricity. I opened my eyes and looked at him as he sank on to the edge of the bed beside me, and I took his hand.

"Kabir, I missed you so much," I told him, lifting his hand to my mouth and brushing my lips across it. He smiled down at me.

"I missed you too," he agreed, and he lay down in the bed next to me, seemingly reading what my desire was for and willing to indulge it. He ran his hand up the length of my waist, tracing the curve where it met my hip, and I felt as though he was wiping clean the memories of Shekhar and everything he had done to me. I knew they would always be there, at the back of my mind, but when Kabir touched me, he made them feel unimportant, secondary, as though they didn't define me.

I moved towards him and placed my hands on his chest, feeling the beat of his heart under his shirt, and even though I knew I was physically exhausted, I felt this surge of energy at being so close to him, at wanting so much from him. I gazed up and into his eyes, and found him staring back at me with an intent that made something in my stomach kindle to life. I remembered the first time, on the couch after that movie, when I had been so scared and so desperate for him in the same breath. And this time, I only felt that desire. I wanted him more intensely than I'd ever wanted anyone in my life before.

"Aamna," he murmured, reaching up to cup my face with his hand. "We don't have to do anything tonight if you don't want to. We can just cuddle, or I can run you a bath..."

"No," I shook my head. "I want... you. I want this."

I shifted again, drawing our faces together, and planted a kiss on his lips. He tasted so good, so familiar, and at once I felt whatever had burned to life inside me growing, filling me, swelling to consume me in the best possible way. As soon as our lips met, he deepened our embrace, moving his hand back to grasp my head and pull me towards him. His tongue was in my mouth, his legs tangled with mine. I hooked my leg over his and pressed my hips against him, surprised and delighted to find him already growing hard beneath his trousers.

"I want you so badly," he growled in my ear, and the words were hypnotic. I felt myself move into that state, that delicious state where only he mattered to me, where his body and mine were the only important things left in the whole universe.

"I want you too," I murmured back, and he moved his mouth from mine and began to kiss down my chin, across my neck, his teeth bearing slightly at my throat. I closed my eyes and tipped my head back, grabbing him and pulling him on top of me, desperate to feel the weight of him holding me down, keeping me earthbound.

His hands moved hungrily all over my body, as though he was reminding himself exactly how I felt to him. He pushed up my skirt, letting his hands slip over my thighs and grip deep into my flesh, and then started on my torso, unbuttoning the top I was wearing swiftly and tossing it aside. Shekhar had purchased the clothes for me, and I would happily have set fire to them at once. It certainly felt right that I was letting another man rip them off me, a man I actually wanted, actually desired.

"Mmm..." Kabir traced his mouth down my neck again and this time continued down to my breasts. He drew each one of my nipples into his mouth in turn, sucking softly until they swelled beneath his lips. I reached down to hold him in place, running my fingers through his soft hair, reminding myself how he felt, every part of him.

He kissed across my stomach, to that sensitive spot just below my navel that seemed to unlock some dark place within me. His hands were busy working at my skirt, pulling it down and letting me kick it aside. And, from them, he slid down between my legs, hooking his fingers over the hips of my underwear and grinning up at me.

"Can I?" He murmured. I looked at his soft mouth and felt a shiver run through me. I nodded.

"Please," I whispered back, and he slowly pulled my underwear from my legs and tossed it aside, so that I was bare naked in front of him. Before any other man, I might have pulled back, tried to hide myself, but I felt no urge to do that with him. His eyes took in every inch of me as he pushed himself up on the bed, staring down at me as though he couldn't believe that I was really here in front of him.

"You're so beautiful," he murmured, and he swiftly moved up to kiss me on the mouth before he slipped back down between my thighs. I groaned and shifted my hips against the bed, my sex already aching for the feel of him, any part of him that he would give me.

He ran his mouth up the length of my thigh, teasing me, his breath warm and eager as he pushed my legs apart. I knew that I should have closed my eyes and let the pleasure take me, but I wanted to watch him as he did this. I wanted to remind myself that the man pleasuring me this way was one that I wanted there, one who had asked to be there. That was the most important thing to me, the sexiest one – that I had given him my consent. That was something sacred that had been silent in my sex life for so long.

He kissed across my belly again and brushed his fingers through my pubic hair. By now, I was pulsing with need, the desire coming out from between my legs to spread all through my body. My teeth were gritted and my body racked with tension as I silently urged him onward, and finally, finally, he lowered his mouth to me for the first time.

"Ah!" I cried out, the sensation at once taking control of me and wiping everything else from my mind. He flattened his tongue and found my most sensitive spot, and stroked at it gently, sending tremors all the way through my body. I reached down to grasp his hair, to hold him in place so he wouldn't go anywhere and began to rock my hips back against him. I felt greedy for this, for whatever he could give me.

"You taste so good," he murmured, pulling back for a moment and looking up at me; his mouth was slick with my wetness, and the sight of his eyes glowing up at me in the dark from between my thighs was enough to send another spasm of pleasure through my system. He returned to the task at hand, sealing his lips around my nub and sucking softly as he continued to stroke me with his tongue.

His hands roamed all over my body as he did so – across my breasts, my legs, my arms, my stomach, and my backside. It was though he was reclaiming his territory, touching every part of me so that he could say it was his again. And I was more than happy to give myself to him in this way, in any way I could. I wanted him to have me like this. I wanted to be his. I wanted to know that a man as good as him desired me, wanted to claim me.

"Oh…" I groaned, my hands balling into fists on the covers beside me as I felt my pleasure swelling deep down within me. My back arched from the bed and I clutched at the sheets, gripping them so tightly I was sure I would leave the imprint in my hands. I watched him, watched him as he used his tongue and his lips to pleasure me, and I knew in that moment that there wasn't a thing in the world he wouldn't have done to please me. And knowing that, knowing that this man would give himself over to me so utterly and without question, was all I needed to push me over the edge.

I let out a noise even I didn't recognize as the orgasm swept through me, feeling as though someone had lit a forest fire in my belly that swiftly spread to consume everything around it. I was trembling when he pulled his mouth from me, and he moved up on top of me, wrapping me in his arms and holding me close as I waited to come back down to earth.

"Kabir…" I groaned his name into his ear, and he turned and covered my mouth with his. I could taste myself on his lips, and that sent another surge of lust through me. I could feel his hardness against my hip as he lay on top of me, and I knew I wanted to taste him, too.

"Here," I carefully moved him so that he was on his back and I was on top of him. I was distinctly aware of the fact that I was totally naked and he was fully dressed, and I knew I wasn't going to be able to let that pass.

"Let me…" I breathed as I started to unbutton his shirt, my fingers trembling as they skimmed over his bare skin. He lay back and let me undress him, let me take my time. I worked slowly, savouring every inch of newly-exposed flesh as I took off his clothes, running my fingers over every part of him. I adored him. I was never going to let this man be taken from me again, no matter what! Come hell or high water, I would be at his side. Nothing could change that.

I finally pulled off his underwear, and his erection sprang free. I wrapped my fingers around him gently, stroking up and down a couple of times and watching the way the pleasure registered on his face. I wanted to give him what he had given me, wanted to show him what I was capable of.

I brushed my mouth over his stomach and flicked my gaze up to meet his as I lowered my mouth down to him for the first time. I traced my tongue over his tip for a moment before I took all of him, knowing that the sensitive spot would intensify things for him; he groaned, the sound coming from deep down inside him, as I took him into my mouth, let him slide all the way into me.

It was an intoxicating feeling, taking him like that – at once, I was submitting to him and controlling him, and the mix of the two was enough to send shivers down my spine. I ran my hands up the inside of his thighs as I guided my mouth slowly up and down his length, his warmth and his taste spreading across my tongue, comforting. He reached out to brush the hair from my eyes, and I looked up at him and found him gazing down at me with pure adoration in his eyes. I remembered the last time the two of us had been in this bed together, it was when I had left without a second word, and how cruel and pointless that all seemed now. But how distant, too – how far removed from how I felt at that moment. I would never go anywhere again. I wanted to stay by his side for good, and I knew that now, without equivocation.

"You look so good doing that," he murmured, and I could hear the ragged edge to his voice, letting me know that he was growing closer to the edge. I would have happily brought him to climax with my mouth, but he only let me go another few moments before he reached down and pulled me on top of him.

"I want to be inside you," he told me, our bodies blending in the dark edges of the room. "I want to feel you again…"

He grabbed a condom from the bedside drawer and swiftly sheathed himself, and I watched as he covered his length. I ached for him inside me, had been aching for him for what felt like a lifetime by now. I spread my legs and moved on top of him, planting my hands on his chest for leverage, and he held himself steady as I slowly lowered myself all the way down upon him.

"Ah," he growled, reaching up to sink his fingers into my hips and guide me down on top of him. As soon as he was all the way inside me, I felt as though a weight had lifted, a weight I'd had no idea I had even been carrying. My body seemed weightless as I began to move on top of him, as he began to thrust back to meet me, as though I was floating through space, and this man was the only thing that was keeping me connected to the ground.

I moved my hips in small circles, pushing myself down and then lifting up again, teasing him with my movements; he reached out and guided my hand down to my nub, and I didn't need telling twice, beginning at once to stroke myself in time with his thrusts, letting him move into me harder, deeper. I felt as though I was being filled, not just literally, but in some deep emotional sense as well, as though this man was giving me everything I needed.

I wasn't sure how long I made love to him like that; he linked his fingers with my free hand to allow me to push back against him harder, and I could see the tension in his jaw, the need in his eyes as he watched me move upon him. I tipped my head back and closed my eyes; finally letting the blend of sensations move across me, take control of me. I could hardly keep the pleasure in any longer, the feeling of it swelling dangerously, building and building and building until…

"Oh…" I breathed as the orgasm swelled through me once more, the pleasure pulsing in every nerve ending for a moment as it blew up from between my legs across my whole body. My system felt for a moment as though it was spinning out of control, the pleasure the only thing that it could possibly take hold of, and then I returned to my body, landing back down on earth, and I felt Kabir find his own release deep inside me. I watched his face, tremoring for a moment, as he reached his climax, and the sight of it was enough to send another wave of pleasure through my body. It felt as though my pleasure had morphed into his, the connection in our bodies allowing us to exchange it between one another.

He gently lifted me off of him, and then slipped the condom from himself and went to dispose of it. I crashed forward into the bed with a smile on my face, my body spent but happy.

He returned a moment later, the creak in the bed alerting me to his presence, and my eyes flickered open once more and landed on him. I reached out to stroke his hair, reminding myself for what felt like the millionth time that he was really there in front of me, that this was really happening. I was free. And I could spend the rest of my life with him if I wanted. Hell, even my parents approved, which saved me the bother of having to prove to them that the man I had chosen was worthy of our family.

"I can't believe you're really here," he remarked, moving his hand down my arm with a look of marvel on his face. "After all this time…"

"I'm so sorry," I blurted out. "I should never have left. I can see that now—"

"You left?" Kabir furrowed his brow, and I realized that he still had no idea as to what had happened the night that I had been taken once more. He had probably just woken up here, all alone, with no explanation as to where I was or what had happened.

"I..." I shook my head. I knew that I had to tell him, but I had no clue how to admit the truth to him, that it had been my own insecurity that had pushed me out the door, not him.

"Why did you go?" he asked, concerned. "I thought he took you, right from the room..."

"No, he found me out on the street," I confessed, even though it pained me to do so. I took a deep breath, knowing that I owed him at least the truth. He had worked so hard to be with me, the very minimum I could offer him in return was the chance to actually understand what had driven me out of that door in the first place.

"I was up late," I admitted, "in the night. And I saw your phone. I didn't mean to look, but I saw a text from a woman you used to date—"

"Chhaya," he muttered, and he spat her name with such vitriol that it secured the knowledge, in case I needed it, that he had no interest in anyone other than me.

"You saw her?" I asked. The text had been about that, I remembered, about getting together again after years apart.

"Yes, I did," he confessed, and my heart dropped at once. But then he shook his head.

"But all it did was confirm to me that I wanted to be with you," he wound his fingers around mine. "I was so heartbroken after you left, and I thought you'd gone on your own accord, so I figured I had to move on. But I couldn't. Even if I wanted to. That's why I went to find your parents. I thought you were with them, and I wanted at least to say goodbye before I let go of you for good."

"And you don't want to see her again?" I asked. He shook his head at once.

"Not at all," he replied firmly. "I just want to be with you, Aamna."

He was gazing at me, his eyes wide and sincere, and I bit my lip.

"After what happened at the mall, I just thought..." I cut myself off, not sure how to phrase this. "I supposed that you would be better off with someone who was less work, that was it. That you didn't deserve to spend your life running around after me, trying to protect me from myself."

"I've never felt that way," he told me fiercely.

"Even though you actually did have to come and save me?" I pointed out, only half-joking.

"I don't care about that," he replied, brushing a strand of hair back from my face. "I don't care how long it takes for you to feel safe again. I'm here for you. I always will be, Aamna."

I looked at him, and I wanted to believe him so desperately, but there was some part of me that doubted him still. Not his love, but his ability to take me on, to take on all those parts of me that even I hadn't uncovered yet.

"I just felt like I wasn't worthy of you," I continued, the words tumbling from me before I had a chance to stop myself. "After everything I'd been through—"

"Nothing of what you've been through makes me think any less of you," he replied, cutting me off. "I know you might feel that way, but it's not true. I want you. Every part of you. Including your past."

He paused for a moment, as though second-guessing what he was about to say, but then he came out with it anyway.

"And your future."

That was enough to get the last piece of resistance within me to give in, and I felt a smile spread over my face. I wanted a future with him too. I wanted everything with him. All that time I had spent trapped in Shekhar's apartment had been an exercise in realizing how deeply I needed what Kabir had to offer me. His kindness, and his acceptance. His hope and his normality and his ability to share that normality with me. I felt a swell of love in my chest, and while I knew it was soon, I had to share it with him.

"I love you," I told him, and his eyes widened. He didn't hesitate in his response.

"I love you too," he replied, brushing his thumb over my mouth as though tracing the words I had just said against me. I smiled against him, and he leaned forward to kiss me. And as soon as our lips met, it was as though he was rewriting me. I knew it would take a long time, and that I wouldn't be able to let go of everything that had happened to me just like that, but for a moment, in his embrace, I could convince myself it was possible. Likely, even. When he pulled back, his eyes were soft, soft in a way that I craved. I had never known men to be soft with me before I met him, but I was happy to have his kindness, his tenderness. It meant more to me than he would ever know.

"I love you," I repeated again, the words foreign but natural on my mouth. I wanted to say them so many times that they were familiar to me, that I could recite them in my sleep.

"I love you, I love you, I love you," he replied back to me, making me laugh. He pulled me close as I tossed my head back in amusement, and he kissed my neck. And before I knew it, I felt another swell of desire growing for him. And I knew that tomorrow I would have to face up to the consequences of what had happened to me, that I would need to give statements and start counselling and accept help, but for now, all I wanted was for me and Kabir to hide ourselves away from the world for the night and remind ourselves how well we worked together. And that we loved each other. The words played in my mind, bright against the darkness, like the first stars of a long night.

17

Kabir

"Good morning," I greeted Aamna as she made her way through to the living room. She gave me a warm smile, and my heart leapt. She had been here almost a week now, and yet, getting to see her every single day didn't get any less thrilling.

"Good morning," she slipped down onto the couch next to me and snuggled up against me. I closed the laptop I had been working on and put my arm around her. Work could wait. I couldn't think of anything more important than cuddling with her right now. I wondered if the novelty would ever wear off, if I would ever grow tired of having her close to me once more. I adored her presence, the warmth it seemed to bring to the house. When she had been gone, I hadn't realized how cold the place had seemed, how devoid of life. But now she was back, and it felt as though everything was bursting into bloom at once.

"What do you want to do today?" I asked her, and she shrugged and shook her head.

"I just finished my book last night," she informed.

"Good?"

"Brilliant," she grinned. "So I think I'm going to start that one I picked up on Wednesday, you remember?"

"The law one?" I furrowed my brow, trying to remember. Aamna had been purchasing a lot of books lately, and it was hard to keep track of them all.

"Yeah, that's the one," she nodded. "I think I'm going to start reading that. It's just an introduction, but it might be interesting. And then I thought I could go down and spend some time with mum and dad."

"That sounds perfect," I leaned my chin on the top of her head, stroking her hair. She fit into me so perfectly, like she was some other half I hadn't realized I had been missing. "You send my best to them, alright?"

"You should come with me," she suggested. "Not today... but sometime this week. I know they'd like to actually see you, especially now that all the... all of the bad stuff is done with."

She hesitated over the statement, and I could feel that flicker of fear coming off of her. I wanted to wind my arms around her and assure her that it was all going to be alright, that she was with me and she was safe now, but I had already told her that a thousand times over and she didn't need to hear it again. What she required now was the time and the help to work through what had happened, and that didn't involve repetitive platitudes from me.

"When's your first therapy appointment?" I asked her, and she pulled a face.

"Monday," she sighed heavily. "I really don't want to go, but I know I should."

"Why don't you want to go?" I wondered aloud. Rashi had insisted that Aamna should see a counsellor from the shelter for at least a few weeks after everything that had happened to her, and I thought it was a good idea too.

"Talking about myself for an hour?" She wrinkled her nose up. "Sounds boring."

"Well, I think talking about you for an hour would be just fascinating," I replied, and she giggled.

"You suck-up," she teased, and she tilted her head up so she could kiss me. I pushed the laptop from my knees and pulled her closer to me, deepening the kiss at once. I still felt as though I couldn't get enough of her, as though I was an addict constantly craving the more dizzying high. She slipped her hand beneath my shirt, fingers trailing over my skin.

And then the buzzer for the door went. Aamna pulled away from me and nodded her head towards the door.

"You should probably get that," she remarked, and I went to kiss her again.

"Maybe we could forget it for now," I murmured against her mouth. "We could just say we were out..."

"Come on," she pushed me off, laughing. "It could be important. I'm not getting in the way of your life, you know."

"But you're such good procrastination," I groaned as I got to my feet and stretched. I headed over to the door, not sure who it could be. I wasn't expecting anyone, but maybe Rashi was just stopping by for a visit to check in on the two of us, or maybe a cop asking for a clarification on the statements we'd given. I pressed the intercom button and leaned forward to speak.

"Hello?"

"Kabir?"

My stomach dropped to my shoes as soon as I heard the voice on the other end of the line. It was Chhaya. What the hell was she doing here? With everything that had happened over the last month, I had completely forgotten about her threat to stick around in my life, and it had been so long since I had seen her that I had assumed she had lost interest and moved on. No such luck.

"Who's that?" Aamna asked, furrowing her brow.

"It's… shit, it's an ex-girlfriend." I shook my head, and her face dropped.

"What?"

"The one who sent me the text…" I admitted, "The one who I was seeing while you were away."

"What's she doing here?" Aamna demanded, wrapping her arms around herself protectively.

"I have no idea," I shook my head. "I can send her away if you want—"

"No, let her in," Aamna told me firmly. I hesitated over the button for a moment, not sure if this was a good idea. I didn't want to make Aamna feel insecure in the face of someone as glamorous as Chhaya – but then, maybe if Chhaya saw that Aamna was here and I was firmly involved with someone else, she would get the message and back off.

"Alright!" I nodded, and I pressed the button to buzz her into the villa. I still wasn't sure this was a great idea, but maybe it would put an end to all this Chhaya nonsense once and for all.

Aamna dipped down behind the back of the couch nervously, hovering just out of sight, as though she didn't want Chhaya to see her. I was going to grab her and have her by my side when I opened the door, but before I could, Chhaya was already there.

"Hello?" she cooed through the door, and I grimaced, steeled myself, and pulled it open. And my jaw dropped when I saw what she was wearing.

She was dressed in a long black jacket, with intricate dark lingerie being the only thing she had on underneath. Suspenders, lacy underwear, a push-up bra, stockings, the whole nine yards. Her hair was teased out around her head, and she had a triumphant expression on her face, obviously reading my shock as desire.

"Well?" She stepped over the threshold and pressed her hands against my chest. "Do you want me now?"

"Chhaya, I don't—"

"Oh, come on, Kabir," she teased, stroking her fingers down my face. She was wearing large fake nails, and they scratched against my skin. I jerked away from her.

"No, Chhaya," I told her firmly, pulling the jacket back around her to cover her up. Nothing about this appealed to me, and I knew that for sure now. Even with her laying herself out for me like a birthday gift, I couldn't imagine anything I wanted less than to touch her like that.

"What?" Her face fell. I had made my feelings clear, and she was the one ignoring that.

"I'm sorry," I shook my head, not sure why I was apologizing. "You need to leave."

"What the hell are you talking about?" her face had twisted now, a mask of anger. "You're seriously telling me you don't want this?"

"I am," I nodded.

"Why not?" She demanded.

"Me."

Chhaya's eyes widened and she turned to see Aamna standing up off the couch and walking over to join me. Her face was drawn and clearly a little shaken by what was going on, but she was firm. Chhaya buttoned her jacket up quickly and glared at me.

"You didn't tell me you were seeing someone else."

"It was complicated," I told her, sliding my arm around Aamna's waist as she approached. "But it's not anymore."

"You're really dating this… girl?" Chhaya waved her hand at Aamna derisively. "When I'm right here?"

"She's a grown woman," I corrected her. "And yes, I am. I told you, I'm not interested in you. It wouldn't work between us."

Chhaya was glancing between us, her brain clearly going at a mile a minute as she tried to find some way out to talk herself out of this. A flush of red was flooding up her neck and over her cheeks, and she was clearly humiliated.

"You really think I wanted you?" She sneered at me suddenly. I raised my eyebrows.

"You're the one who turned up here dressed like that," I pointed out, and Aamna let out a little splutter of laughter, burying her face into my shoulder to keep it in. Chhaya's eyes blackened, like smoldering coals.

"You thought you were so clever, playing hard to get," she shook her head. "I didn't want you, Kabir. Did you really think I'd come crawling back to you after the way things ended?"

"Then what the hell were you doing?" I furrowed my brow. I could tell she was just trying to save face, but some part of me was curious about what her reasoning was for this, if not desire for me.

"You heard about my father, no doubt," she rolled her eyes. "Lost all our money. Typical man. Can't think about anything but himself and his own selfish pleasure."

"What?" I raised my eyebrows. I'd heard some murmurs about the state of her family, but they must have been keeping that information carefully close to their chests.

"I have a lifestyle, Kabir," she ignored my question. "I have a life that I'm used to. And if he's not able to uphold it—"

"You were just going to try to get close to me for the money?" I finished up for her bluntly. She closed her mouth, and I could tell that hearing the words come out of my mouth so harshly had taken her off-guard. But still, she pressed on.

"We make sense together, Kabir," she told me haughtily. "We're from the same place in the world. Not like…"

She waved her hand at Aamna, who stiffened next to me. I felt a swell of anger at Chhaya for daring to speak to her like that. I knew how insecure Aamna was about not being worthy of me, of this life, and the thought of Chhaya deciding to add to that made me even more furious.

"Don't speak to her like that," I snapped back. "She's twice the woman you'll ever be."

"Oh, really," Chhaya drawled. "I think I heard about you. Aamna, right? You were in the news."

"Yes, that's me," Aamna murmured, and I could tell she was doing her best to keep her voice from wavering. I wanted to grab her hand and look into her eyes and tell her to ignore Chhaya, but Aamna was regarding her with a steady gaze, as though she wanted to hear what she had to say.

"You're the whore, aren't you?" Chhaya remarked, and she laced the word with a syrupy sweetness, as though trying to deflect any anger I might have thrown her way for speaking to Aamna like that. But she wasn't going to slide that by me. "Your parents know?" She arched her eyebrows at me and I knew what she was going to do. She was going to run with this news and break it to my parents. Well, I would deal with them when I would have to…

"You have no idea what you're talking about," I pushed my face closer to hers, my jaw tensing as I stared her down. "Aamna has been through things you could never imagine. And she's still a better person than you'll ever be."

"Just because you want to play the hero with some broken woman—"

"It's got nothing to do with that," Aamna snapped, invading the conversation with her sharp words. "Kabir isn't doing this to be a hero. He's…"

She looked at me, and her gaze softened and I felt something in me give as well. Where a moment before I had wanted nothing more than to scream at Chhaya for speaking to Aamna in that way, I felt the urge to tell her off drifting away, slipping out of focus. I didn't care what she had to say. I didn't care what anyone had to say. As long as Aamna was by my side, their words would just slide off of me.

"I love her," I told Chhaya. "I love her, and that's all that matters. I don't care about her past, and I don't care who she is or where she came from – I love her. In a way, I could never love you."

Chhaya's face flashed with fury once more, and I knew that she was already planning another attack on the two of us, but I didn't care to hear it. Before she could open her mouth, I closed the door in her face and listened until I heard her footsteps stamping back downstairs and out into the street once more. I let out a long breath as soon as she was gone, and turned to Aamna, who had her eyebrows raised in surprise.

"I'm so sorry about that," I shook my head. "Don't listen to a word she says. She has no idea what she's talking about."

"Do you think that's how people see me?" she murmured, voice tiny and sucked off all the spike that she had addressed towards Chhaya. "A whore?"

"They might," I conceded, and her eyes drooped towards the floor. I touched her chin to draw her gaze back up to me. "But it doesn't matter."

"How not?" she looked at me hopefully, clearly searching for the promise of some relief from her insecurities.

"Because what happened to you has made you who you are," I told her. "I know, if I could go back in time and change it, I would. I would take it all away from you and carry it myself if I was able to. But the woman you are now, you're a result of what you went through. You survived."

"I survived," she repeated after me, as though it was only really just sinking it at that moment.

"It doesn't define your future," I continued. I didn't even realize I'd thought about all this stuff myself, but I supposed that Aamna was always ticking over at the back of my mind, even when I wasn't aware of it.

"You're not worried that's how people will look at me?" she asked, eyes wide. "That people will just think of me… think of me in that way?"

"I don't give a damn what people think of you", I replied fervently. "I only care what I think of you. And I love you."

"I love you too," she murmured, and she clasped my face and kissed me, smiling against my mouth. I caught hold of her waist and pulled her close, feeling the effervescence in her spirit passing from her mouth to mine.

"I'm sorry," she pulled back and shook her head. "I don't want… I know I'm insecure. Sometimes, I think you should be with someone more…"

"You're the only person I need," I told her firmly. "I know you might have a hard time believing that sometimes, but I don't."

"You'll just have to believe hard enough for the both of us." She managed a smile.

"No problem at all," I assured her, and I took her hand. "You want to go out to get some breakfast?"

"Don't you have work to do?" she glanced back towards my computer.

"It can wait." I shrugged. "I'd rather be showing you off around the city."

"Well, I don't think I can say no to that," she said and giggled. "Just let me get to showing-off ready, alright?"

"You already are," I pointed out, and she blushed a little.

"Stop it," she warned me. "Or else you're going to get my head so swollen that I would have trouble getting it through the door."

"Just means I could keep you all to myself," I teased as she headed through to the bedroom to get dressed, and she waved her hand at me over her shoulder and closed the door behind her. I leaned back against the wall and found myself staring at the spot she had just left.

I knew that some people were going to question our relationship – Chhaya wouldn't be the first or the only person assuming I was playing the hero by taking her in. But before, where I might have taken into account the way other people looked at my choice of partner, now I knew that it didn't matter. My heart was full; my life, for the first time, felt the same. Aamna, no matter what anyone else thought of her, was the person I had always been searching for. I never could have imagined in a million years that I would end up with someone who had been through as much as she had, but none of that mattered. It had made her the woman she was – compassionate, brave, intuitive, open, hopeful. Her past only mattered to me as far as I could help her overcome it, and I would never judge her for what she had endured.

And, as she healed, I knew she might change. But I also knew that I was in love with some deep part of her soul, and no matter the person she became, that wasn't going to change. She would never stop making sense to me. And, surely, nothing else in the world mattered.

Epilogue

Aamna

One year later…

Dear Aamna,

It feels strange, writing this letter to you. Well, to me, I suppose – but now I don't feel that I am the same person as I was five years ago. The time when they had taken you, i.e., me. So much has changed over time that now I think of you as a whole separate person most of the time.

I still think writing this letter is a silly idea, even though my therapist says it's a good one. And she's not led me wrong so far, so I guess I am going to get along with it and see what happens.

Where do I start? Firstly, I'm sorry. I'm sorry you had to go through all that in that hell-hole. I'm sorry I didn't do more to protect you. I'm sorry you're where you are right now, and I'm sorry you're suffering in the most brutal way. I'm sorry, I really am, and I know that right now it seems like it's never going to end, but it will. Sometimes, you'll feel like there's nothing on the other side of this for you, but I promise you that there is.

I wish I could trace out to you the path you'll go down that will lead you to where I am now. But if I'm being honest with you, I barely remember most of it. I know that it happened, I was freed, but it was all such a rush and such a shock that my brain never really had a chance to take it in. All that I know is that I got out and that I met Kabir.

Kabir Oberoi. If I could go back in time and implant the idea of him in your head, I would do it, because I don't think either of us ever believed that we are even going to find someone like him. I know that right now, trapped there, you think there are no good men out there in the world – and you have plenty of reasons to believe that. Trust me, I know, but Kabir is one of them. He is the good one, and he proves that from the first moment you meet him, when he takes you in without a second thought, giving you a place in his home and, not long afterwards, his heart.

At first, you might doubt your love for Kabir – no, that's not true. You'll doubt his love for you. You'll doubt that someone like him could ever truly love somebody who's been broken the way you have been. And those thoughts will start to take root in your head, and you'll run away, terrified of inflicting your damage on him. You don't want to drag him down with you. And I get it. He's the kind of man we both dreamed of when we were little – kind, funny, charming, compassionate, brave, dedicated. You'll wonder if you deserve him, if you'll ever believe that you deserve him. And you do. And you will. I promise.

The year after you get free – and there will be some backsliding, courtesy of Shekhar, who will end up locked up within a matter of months after you escape – it's going to be a hard one. I'm here now, just at the end of it, and sometimes I look back and wonder how on earth I did it. I started going to therapy, reluctantly at first, but soon enough I realized that I was going to need to if I was going to heal myself. Sometimes, the darkness in you would feel like it is stretching out into infinity and you'll fear that you'll never find the other side of it, but you will find ways to navigate that pain and to make something of it. Kabir will help. He will be your lifeboat in the pitch-black, and he will do everything he can to help carry you through it.

Kabir. I keep talking about Kabir. Did I mention that we're engaged now? See, life does take good turns, and eventually, you will be becoming Aamna Oberoi from Aamna Nagpal.

It's still so new that I keep on having to remind myself that he really asked me to marry him. It was the perfect proposal; he took me for a long walk in the forest, far from the rest of the world, popping a bottle of wine next to a river and toasting to me before he produced a ring from his pocket. He didn't even have the words out before I said yes. He laughed and slipped the ring on to my finger, and I stared at it and then him and haven't stopped doing either since.

I know that you're wondering about it – sex. If I'm getting married to a man, then I must be having sex with him, right? Well, yes. And I know that the thought of sex might scare you right now because your sex life has felt like it hasn't belonged to you ever. They took you as a virgin and then corrupted you in the worst possible way. I know your body doesn't feel as though it's yours anymore, it feels as if it belongs to the world at large, that any pleasure you might get from it has been commodified and sold off and stripped from you. I know that you often feel like you exist outside of your body, that you have to remove your spirit from your physical form to survive, but you will begin to reconnect those two sides, the circuits sparking back into life, slowly but surely. It will take hard work, but it will be worth it. Sex with Kabir will remind you what it feels like to want again, to feel true, organic desire that doesn't exist within the boundaries of what has been forced on you. I promise.

Your parents will accept you back with open arms. I know that's a worry you struggle with all the time, and it makes sense – how many people would be willing to accept someone so broken and defiled back into their lives? But your parents don't see you like that. They never do. Some people out there will treat you that way, as if you are irrevocably broken, but you are not, and your family wants you to remember that. You have years to catch up on with them, and your mother will guide you through the worst of it. Those days when you need to weep in her arms, she will be there to hold you, to remind me of all that you have survived so far. You will fall in love with your family again, and you will be grateful that they waited for you.

And don't worry, you will move far away from the city it happened in, too. After a few months in Delhi, Kabir is going to get restless, and his work at the Delhi office will come to a close, and he will suggest that the two of you move back to his hometown, Chandigarh. And you will agree without a second thought. Of course, you miss your parents, but Kabir promises for them to visit any time you'd like. Did I mention that Kabir's family is rich? Well, they are, and that makes everything a lot easier. Your parents come and visit whenever they want – almost monthly. They love Kabir, almost as much as you do, and they treat him like a son. Your father will tease him about not asking permission to marry you, and Kabir will point out that you are your own woman and that my father has no say in who you marry. You will see your mother giggling at that behind dad's back and feel elated.

Speaking of parents, you will move in with Kabir's mother and father, Harish and Sushma. You are going to meet them a couple of times before you move there, and you will sometimes wonder if they like you; at your worst, you let your mind drift back to the time when they will barge into the villa and demand an explanation from Kabir. They know what happened to you – it was reported pretty widely, and they will find it very hard to accept. This is going to happen soon after Kabir's ex came to the villa and told him that she was better suited to him than I was. Kabir never imagined that she was going to tattle everything to his parents, but apparently, she did. Kabir will ask you to stay in Kabir's room, but curious as you always are, you will listen to their conversation.

It is not a pleasant one. Kabir's parents throw in a fit because he is dating a 'whore', but Kabir retaliates. His parents will blackmail him emotionally, psychologically and even threaten to disinherit him, but he is not going to budge. He loves you to his core and will refuse to let you go. His parents will not accept you that day, but Kabir will play it tactfully. He will give them time to think and process the news. And well, as you already know that you will be engaged in future, his parents do eventually accept you – with grave difficulty, but they are going to.

Rashi will be a big part in Kabir's parents accepting you. They will visit the shelter, at her insistence, and when they come back, they will be different. You'll wonder what she said to them, what she did to change their minds, but you'll decide not to look into it too deeply. Suffice to say, his mother greets you with a warm hug every time she comes back from the shelter, and Kabir beams at you over her shoulder.

Rashi will visit often and you will travel back to Delhi to continue your therapy there. You and Rashi will become fast friends, which you find incredible, as you never much got on with women before. But Rashi is not like any girl you ever met. She is different – she is bold and funny and unapologetic, and you meet a lot of women like her at the shelter. You find yourself surrounded by kindness and it feels better than you ever could have imagined. And seeing all those amazing women doing such incredible work to save women from the same nightmare that you were stuck in will inspire you. Why wouldn't it? You will want to join them, but a feeling of helplessness will creep within you. You will feel that 'when you are still trying to put yourself back together, how can you help other women?' You occasionally will catch a glimpse of a woman brought into the shelter, one who has just been liberated from an abusive relationship or sex trafficking, and you will feel a sharp twist in your gut like someone has forced a knife between your ribs. You recognize the look on their faces: helpless, hopeless, trying to imagine a future without the abuse and coming up with nothing. When you express this to Kabir, and he will be nervous, at first – you will understand why, as you have worked so hard to get where you are and this feels like plunging head-first back into the bad dream that trapped you for so long. But you know that one day you want to turn your experiences into something useful, something worthwhile, and in future, you will begin to try and work out how you might do that.

You will read law books constantly, and you find it so fascinating, even though everyone else seems to treat them as dry academia. Eventually, it will hit you – you should go to university and study law. You will think about what you could bring to these women who are terrified of pressing charges against their abusers, and it fills you with a determination you have never felt before in your life. You know this is what you have to do. You apply for university, and you're pretty sure that it's the interview that gets you in. You speak passionately to the admissions officer, and you notice them looking over articles about you as you speak, and by the time you walk out of there, you have been accepted to study at Chandigarh University. The course will be long and hard, but you're ready for it. In fact, things won't always feel as easy as that. Sometimes, things will feel impossible. The work will be too hard, and you will begin to doubt your ability to actually make any kind of change. Even when Shekhar is locked away for the rest of his life, you'll feel not triumph, but an overwhelming sense of horror – at the knowledge that you had to go through all of this for one man to be taken off the streets, a man who had inflicted so much on so many women, and that there are so many more men out there doing the same thing to women just like you. You'll wonder if this is worth it. The future will stretch out in front of you and, instead of hope, sometimes you will be shaken by the sheer amount of things you want to do, as if you are running out of time. And that makes sense. Years were taken from you, and you are trying to catch up on that lost time. Don't beat yourself up over it. It's a normal way to feel.

Sometimes, staring your past in the face will make you want to crawl out of your own skin. It would make you so desperate that you will feel as though you could crawl your way out of your own body just to escape from what's going on in your head. Those times will become less and less as time goes on, but it's unlikely that they will ever go away. I know that I am only a year out from this, though, and I have hope that one day I will live my life and barely give a thought to what I went through. But just so you know: the pain is part of the healing. You have to look at the agony in the face to understand it, and you will come to understand it better and better as time passes. And there will be other times when the future looks so hopeful that it will make your heart hurt. Right now, stuck in that hell-hole, you're probably struggling to imagine anything beyond the next few hours, and I get that – to look forward would be to accept that there is nothing for you in that place and that the chances of you finding a way out are slim. But it will come. I know there is still that flicker of hope in the back of your mind, and soon it will bloom into a flame.

Kabir and I have talked a lot about starting a family. I want to finish my degree first and get a few good years behind me in the industry before I settle down, but I know that I want it. That must sound crazy to you – you feel so far removed from your own family at the moment that you're struggling to imagine even loving yourself again, let alone a family of your own. But family will come to you, and you will feel as though you have found so many connections that it's natural for you to want to make some more of your own. You will have your own family back, you will have Kabir's family, and most of all, you will have Kabir – because being with him feels like home. When you hold his hand, a weight always lifts from your shoulders, and you know that you are not carrying all this alone. And you are not.

This letter has already gone on for so long. I didn't realize how much I had to say to you. I wonder if I'll write a letter to myself in five years' time, and look back and see that things have changed so much once again. In fact, I know I'll do that. I can't wait to see where I am in a few years from now, the changes I've made, both to myself and the world around me.

I guess if there is one thing I want to say to you, it's this: it gets better. And I know that if today I go back in time and say that to your face, you will laugh at me and dismiss me out of hand, and I get it. But it will get better. Time will heal you, and love will, too. Therapy will help. A purpose will guide you. And what you have been through will drive you forward and inform the choices you make, give you a sense of urgency that you will come to love about yourself. But most of all, you will become yourself again. Now, you feel so different from the person you thought you were, so much so that you can barely remember who she was in the first place. You will reclaim yourself. You will fall in love with yourself, and you will accept that you are worthy of love from others, too. And sometimes, just sometimes, you will look at yourself in the mirror in the morning, while Kabir is beside you, carefully shaving for work, and you will smile at yourself. And you feel a wash of complete, pure contentment. It won't last forever, but the memory of it never fades. And you will hold on to those moments, and they will be enough to remind you that you can and will survive whatever is thrown at you.

I love you. And you're going to make it through.

Aamna